The Jizmatic Trilogy

+

(annotated edition)

MICHAEL ANDRE-DRIUSSI

"Under the Moons of Jizma" was first published in
Interzone 110, August 1996.

CONTENTS

I   Under the Moons of Jizma   1

II   The Gods of Jizma   43

III   Secret Master of Jizma   81

Under the Moons[1] of Jizma[2] (a Scientific Romance)

---

1. *A Princess of Mars* by Edgar Rice Burroughs (hereafter "ERB") was originally published serially as "Under the Moons of Mars" in *All-Story Magazine* in 1912.

2. Jizma: Derived from "jism," a word meaning energy, spirit, or spunk. Presumably the name for a land or world of high energy or greater spirit. ERB gave his Mars the name "Barsoom," which has a mysterious origin, but looks to be "B" for "Burroughs" plus "pig Latin" Mars as "Arsoom." While the name initially seems exotic, over time Barsoom looks rather too much like "barroom."

FOREWORD

To the Reader of this Work:

In submitting Doctor Lee's curious manuscript to you, I believe a few notes are in order. First of all, even though my uncle Doctor Lee has been legally pronounced deceased as of last year, I cannot be certain that he will not visit me tomorrow. Secondly, among my inheritance from him was a thick sheaf of handwritten pages, un-numbered, and varying greatly in legibility. So while I am not, strictly speaking, the author of this tale, it would be dishonest of me to claim that I was not its editor, arranging it into the form you have before you now.

Yours very sincerely,

Norm L. Bean[3] (1912)

---

3. "Under the Moons of Mars" was published with the pen name "Normal Bean." ERB's idea here was to suggest he was a "normal bean," not a cultist. A typesetter corrected it to "Norman Bean." (See Richard A. Lupoff, *Master of Adventure: The Worlds of Edgar Rice Burroughs*, p. 7; Irwin Porges, *Edgar Rice Burroughs: The Man Who Created Tarzan*, p. 136.)

NARRATOR'S PROLOGUE

I am old, rendered ancient beyond my years by the curious adventures I am about to relate. Looking at my withered frame you would be hard pressed to believe that I am only nine and thirty years — I might easily pass for a man twice that age.[4]

I was born in 1857, heir to a modest plantation in Virginia. My inheritance was destroyed before my tenth year by the War, yet my family's pride and sacrifice sent me to Harvard. I graduated in 1879 with a few awards for pistol marksmanship and a degree in Chemistry, following in the footsteps of my late father, a gentleman-scientist of the old school. Upon returning to my ancestral home I was struck with a new appreciation of how much had been lost, and I renewed my determination to rebuild the family fortune.

Eight years went by, during which I obtained a license

---

4. Narrator is preternaturally old-looking. Compare with the opening line of *A Princess of Mars:* "I am a very old man; how old I do not know." Yet the ERB hero eternally appears to be thirty years of age.

and became a pharmacist in a town forgotten by the Reconstruction. My only consolation was the regular correspondence with my college chum Teddy, who was first in New York City, then in the Dakota territory where he sought solace for a few years after losing his wife and his mother, then in New York again. Both of us longed for excitement and felt that life was passing us by — the railroads had already reached the Far West, signaling that the last Heroic Age was almost over.

But then in 1887 I received the call to adventure. My employer, Mr. Bradly Martin,[5] had determined in the course of reading a few volumes of quaint and curious lore[6] that the Age of Alcohol was nearly over and that a brand new world of soft drinks, women's suffrage, and free love was about to dawn.

"Look at Pemberton down in Atlanta," he said. "Coca-Cola. Folks down there are going crazy for it. I am telling you, Will, it is going to get even bigger. Then there is Alderton out in Texas, calls his concoction 'Doctor Pepper.' Hell, I *know* Doc Pepper — he prefers prune juice. You got the Women's Christian Temperance Union over in Ohio pushing for an end to alcohol, and you know it? They are going to win. But people have to drink something, so they will come in here for a soda. We will replace the saloons, get it?

"But we need something special, something new. Root beer just will not cut it. We need a 'secret ingredient.' Ol'

---

5. Mr. Bradly Martin: Reference to "Mr. Bradley Mr. Martin" [sic], a character from the Nova Trilogy of William S. Burroughs (henceforth "WSB"), he is "thought to be the leader of . . . the nova mob" in "the nova police" section (Ch. 6) of *The Ticket That Exploded*.

6. curious lore: A jumbled fragment of the opening to Edgar Allan Poe's poem "The Raven" (1845).

Pemberton is probably using a mite of cocaine in his drink, gives a body a healthy zip. Even the Brits are getting in on this — look at Schweppes and their tonic water, that has got quinine — malaria medicine. We need something unique, and the key is hidden somewhere in South America. Like the coca plant. The Amazon jungle must be overflowing with undiscovered treasures — who knows what secrets died with the Mayans and the Incas? Ah, if I were only younger, I would set out for adventure to make my fortune . . ." [7]

Wlm. Lee[8] (1896)

---

7. Textual variation: In the *Interzone* text of "Under the Moons of Jizma," Martin uses contractions "I'm," "it's," "there's," "They're," "they'll," "ain't," "that's," and "I'd." However, this is not up to ERB code.

8. William Lee: The hero of WSB's novel *Naked Lunch;* see "lazarus go home" section (Ch. 8). Also the pseudonym used by WSB for his first novel *Junkie* (1953).

1 MY ADVENTURE BEGINS

The mighty Amazon, Father of all Rivers, snaking through a colossal jungle so dark-green as to be almost black. At Belém I caught a steamboat heading upriver. I could feel the heat closing in[9] every time the sun rose, and the equatorial humidity made the air so thick I thought I might swim in it. I felt as though, instead of going to the center of a continent, I were about to set off for another world entirely. I badly missed Teddy, sorry that he could not join me on this trip.

Nearly a week later I arrived at Manaós, in the heart of the jungle. It is the only major city within six hundred miles and was experiencing an economic boom in wild rubber. That was my cover story — should anybody ask, I was there to harvest rubber; but the place was so full of adventurers and fortune-hunters that I felt I could pass amongst them unnoticed.

My Portuguese was even worse than my Spanish, however, so I sought out a physician in the hopes that his

---

9. The opening line of *Naked Lunch* begins "I can feel the heat closing in . . . ," referring to police action that seems imminent.

English (or Latin, should it come to that) would prove sufficient for communication. As luck would have it, I found a Doctor Monygham.[10]

"I would guess, *senhor*," he said, after I had introduced myself, "that you have not come to Manaós for the *borracha,* the rubber, eh? You search instead for the medicine, do you not?"

My surprise must have been immediately evident, since he laughed out loud.

"How could you . . . ?" I asked.

"You come from a good family," he explained. "Not like these vermin. You are a man of science, like me. But most important, you lack the gleam of gold in your eye. Besides, you are not working for Madame Sosostris."[11]

"'Sosostris'?" The name sounded vaguely familiar. I thought of Mr. Martin Bradly's[12] small library.

"*Não tem importancia,* even if you are, I tell you the same thing. Here, take the easy one and go back home. There is a vine called by the savages 'Yage' or 'Ayuahuaska'; our term is *bannisteria caapi.*[13] It is a powerful narcotic — the medicine men use it for visions. Who knows? It may be the next morphine. Dried samples are totally inert, so take some vine clippings back to your home and plant them."

---

10. Monygham: A bitter, eccentric character in Joseph Conrad's novel *Nostromo* (1904), set in a fictitious nation of South America.

11. Madame Sosostris: Reader of fortune-telling cards in T.S. Eliot's "The Waste Land" (lines 43 to 59).

12. Martin Bradly: Previously given in this text as Bradly Martin.

13. Yage: Mentioned in *Naked Lunch* appendix "Letter from a Master Addict to Dangerous Drugs," it was the object of WSB's two-month side trip to the Amazon in 1951.

"You said that was the easy one. What else is there?"

"The hard one. It is like chasing a ghost . . . "

"What is it?"

The doctor sighed. "There is a legend that far to the south of here there is an old medicine woman called Lupita.[14] She lives in a cave and has ancient knowledge. But this is only a legend."

"I choose the hard way," I said. "I must find Lupita."

"But remember Ponce de Leon," said the doctor. "He too chased after a legend, and paid for it with his life."

"Schliemann found Troy nearly twenty years ago, doctor, but until that time it was thought to be only legendary as well. Can you help me find Lupita?"

"Yes, I will do what I can," he said. "It will cost money, but it will cost more than that, much more." From a desk drawer he withdrew a large pair of calipers. "I always ask leave, in the interests of science, to measure the crania of those going out there . . . "[15]

"And when they come back, too?"

"Oh, I never see them," he said. "Besides, the changes take place inside, you know." He smiled, as if at some quiet joke.

After jotting down the measurements, he advised me to go back to the hotel and promised to send someone for me in a few days.

---

14. Lupita: A criminal figure introduced in *Naked Lunch* (Ch. 3) section "the rube," as follows: "Mexico City where Lupita sits like an Aztec Earth Goddess."

15. calipers: This seems a reference to John Fowles, *The Magus*, Chapter 15, p. 80, wherein the eccentric host Conchis measures the hero Urfe's head.

2 AT THE HEART OF DARKNESS[16]

My guide was dead, I was nearly out of bullets, and the nameless jungle savages were gaining on me. Blindly I crashed through the overgrowth, seeking higher ground to make my last stand. As I scrambled up the steep slope of a hill, arrows began to rain down around me, so when a cave mouth appeared I gratefully dove into it. Frantically I reloaded my S&W Safety Hammerless revolver for the last time and waited for the attack. The longest minutes of my life went by, but the attack did not come.

I heard a scuffling sound in the cave behind me and turned to see a weird, macabre sight. There was a tripod filled with a coarse powder that gave off an eerie phosphorescent glow, and beside this was some kind of couch with a pile of rags upon it. Glancing around I noticed at least a dozen bundles of honeycomb that had obviously been brought here by others, and I surmised that this chamber must be some sort of temple or shrine.

After I had taken a few steps closer I realized that the 'rags' I had seen were actually the mummified remains of a

---

16. Reference to Joseph Conrad's novel *Heart of Darkness* (1902).

woman lying upon the couch, arms and legs akimbo. The corpse was naked except for some elaborate jewelry, and her shriveled lips exposed long yellow canines — could this be 'Lupita,' the little she-wolf?

I turned to examine the glowing powder more closely. As I reached in to pick some up, the pile shifted and I suddenly found a foot-long centipede wrapped around my arm, its head in my fist, its tail whipping around searching for purchase.

When the stinger struck home there was a moment of pain followed by a wave of heat spreading from my arm throughout my body. I threw the centipede away from me and noticed a few others already scurrying around. Despite this, a sense of delicious dreaminess overcame me, and my muscles relaxed. Unable to stand, I tried to sit upon the couch but ended up sprawling onto it. Even face to face with the grinning horror of Lupita I could do nothing but look away toward the cave mouth. I felt my heartbeat slow. The day went by in what seemed to be only a few minutes; the night went by even faster as my heartbeat continued to slow until finally, sometime before dawn, it stopped altogether. For a moment I stood outside my body, looking down upon it as if from a vantage point on the ceiling. Then there was an instant of extreme cold and utter darkness.

3 THE MASTER MIND OF JIZMA[17]

I must have closed my eyes involuntarily during the transition through the ether, for when I opened them I was lying naked and prone on the cold tiled floor of a small room. A few yards away were the corpses of a boy and girl, both red-skinned and lacking craniums. A hellish baboon-like creature with six limbs seemed to be in the process of devouring their exposed brains, while standing over me with a mystified expression was the strangest looking individual I had ever seen, a man as red as an Indian and as shriveled as Methuselah.

A small, dirty window high up let in a bit of weak light, but the room was well lit by unearthly bars of illumination set in the ceiling. The man, who wore a bloodstained apron like that of a butcher, spoke to me in an unintelligible language that sounded for all the world like the various noises that insects make. I watched in horror as the baboon-thing scooped out the brains of first one corpse, then the other, dropping them to lie upon the

17. Reference to ERB novel *The Master Mind of Mars* (1928), sixth in the Martian series.

filthy floor. The man continued trying to communicate with me, shifting into a variety of languages that sounded vaguely like Arabic or Greek. Finally he said, *"Sprechen Sie Deutsch?"*

"No," I responded, sitting up. "I speak English."

His eyes lit up. The ghoul beside him noticed me for the first time and bared its prodigious teeth.

"Ah, English," said the man, gesturing the creature to step aside. "Very like German, yes? Me, Herr Doctor Benway,"[18] he thumped his chest. "This" — he gestured to the ghoul — "is mine assistant, Hovan."[19] The beast touched its forehead and bowed. "And *du?* Who are you?"

"I am William Lee."

"Wiggle'em Lie?"

"No, William Lee."

"Too hard. I call you Will," he said. "You mind I work?"

I had no answer, so he squatted down and picked up the boy's brain. "Very good. Now please to tell me where from you come?"

"I am from Virginia," I said.

"Va-jinya, Va-jinya," he mused as he put the brain into

---

18. Doctor Benway: Subject of *Naked Lunch* (Ch. 4) section "benway."

19. Hovan Du: A character from *Master Mind of Mars*, he is half of a human brain in the body of a white ape, thus a man/ape. More of this happens in *Synthetic Men of Mars* (1940), where one synthetic man named Tor-dur-bar becomes "Tun-gan" when his brain is transplanted into the body of Gantum-Gur, and (Vor Daj) when Vor Daj's brain is put into Tor-dur-bar's body. WSB's *The Soft Machine* (Nova Triology #1) has many cases of mix and match surgical hybridization, for example in "The Mayan Caper," where the time travel agent and the young Mayan are split vertically and recombined as a new composite.

the girl's body and drove a strange silver instrument up a nostril of the corpse. "No, I have never heard of that place." He twiddled the instrument around several times, then turned to re-attach the cranium with what appeared to be a kind of glue.

"It is in America," I offered.

"Never heard of that place either. No matter, many places I know not. So, Will, what can I do you for?" When I failed to answer, he added, "And how did you manage to get in through the locked door, anyway?"

"I woke up here."

"The room was empty before, and the door is still locked," he said as he performed the same operation on the other corpse. "What, are you some kind of *gigim*? A ghost?" He looked up in surprise. "Is that what your name is, Will Gigim?"

"No, I am not a ghost — at least, I do not think I am."

"Well you look pale enough to be a *gigim*," he said, continuing at his labor. "Maybe you are sick. Or maybe you just need a new body. I would have to charge you full-price, since the resale value of the one you have now would be virtually nil — except as a curiosity, perhaps."[20]

"No," I said. "I am happy with the body I have now."

After resealing the second skull, he stood up and stretched.

"Nurse, sew them up, revive them, and get them out of here. Our rental time runs out. Meet us back at the house when you are through." To me he said, "Come along." He unlocked the door. "We can look among new bodies for

20. Body exchange: In *The Master Mind of Mars*, scientist Ras Thavas transplants brains of rich elderly Martians into young bodies of hapless victims. The action in the text here seems a match for chapter one of *The Master Mind of Mars*, where the newly arrived Earthman witnesses such a procedure. Body exchange is also a central element to WSB's *The Soft Machine*.

you, if nothing else."

I hesitated.

"Surly you cannot stay here," he said. "And where else do you have to go?"

There was truth in what he said, so I followed him into a cavernous room bustling with well-armed red men and women all scantily clad with leather harnesses. The women were as willowy and lissome as adolescent girls. I hid my nakedness until my patron lent me his apron to wear.

We boarded a bullet-shaped vehicle that apparently operates on the pneumatic principle, travelling in excess of one hundred miles per hour to emerge in another cavernous room roughly forty-five minutes later. Following Benway's example, I leapt over a little hurdle and jogged behind him up a ramp spiraling to the surface where a stunning vision stopped me in my tracks: for there was the Moon, but it was too small; and even as I grappled with this intelligence, another moon, even smaller, shot across the sky.

"Where is this place?" I ejaculated, bewildered by the slender towers and the eggshell domes.

"Why, Annexia,[21] of course," said Benway. "Lesser Freedonia."[22]

"What planet?"

"*Planet?!*" cried Benway. "Do not become spooky on me, Will Gigim. This is planet Jizma, fourth from the Sun."

---

21. Annexia: Mentioned in *Naked Lunch* section "benway." On the ERB side, it seems to be the city-state of Lesser Helium.

22. Freedonia: Perhaps "the Freeland Republic" mentioned in *Naked Lunch* section "benway." On the ERB side, it seems to be based on Greater Helium, the capital of the Heliumatic Empire. Unfortunately it echoes a satiric nation in *Duck Soup* (1933), a motion picture by the Marx Brothers.

4 LINN OF MAVROSIA

I became a part of Benway's mansion menagerie, but once I exhibited my pharmaceutical knowledge I was graduated to staff. The aboveground structure was simple and slightly ruinous; the subterranean chambers held a few dozen bodies heaped about in disarray, preserved by an exotic embalming fluid the composition of which was known only to the Master Mind himself.

Days ran into weeks, weeks into months, as I labored at the side of Benway, and more and more the old surgeon took me into his confidence, imparting to me the secrets of his skill and his profession.[23] I quickly learned the Jiz-matic language, which seems remarkably similar to ancient Greek, but since Hovan lacked the vocal chords necessary for speech I had no one to talk to or confide in.

One day a remarkable creature came to the mansion, a

---

23. Apprentice to mad scientist: In chapter two of *The Master Mind of Mars,* newly arrived Earthman Ulysses Paxton is taken as apprentice by elderly scientist Ras Thavas. Note that here the storyline, ostensibly following *A Princess of Mars,* has been hijacked by that of *The Master Mind of Mars.*

talking *gaidaros*[24] or Jizmatic ass that introduced itself as "Linn" and asked to have audience with Benway. At their meeting, the gold colored gaidaros abased itself before Benway, begging for its former body and shedding copious tears.[25] It was heartbreaking, and I immediately sided with Linn, wondering which of the svelte corpses in the chambers beneath us was hers.

Benway was not moved. "Linn, this was the punishment meted out to you by Ayssa, Empress of Mavrosia. You should not have thwarted Her, or thought that you could do so with impunity. Your attractive body, which She coveted, was taken from you and now you reside in the body of an ass until the end of your days several centuries hence, or until such time as Ayssa commutes your sentence." He paused for a moment, chin in hand. "In the unlikely event that She does grant you such a mercy, you would want to be close at hand in order to quickly regain your old shell. To help you in this, I offer to take you into my stable as a beast of burden, but heed this warning — do not speak to me again of betraying the desires of Ayssa, or I shall turn you out into the world to fend for yourself."

In this manner Linn came to be my constant companion. Her body was not among those in our catacombs, but was kept by the fearful and despotic Ayssa, Queen of a far off land. In the weeks that followed I had seen much of Linn and in our daily intercourse there had been revealed to me little by little the wondrous beauties of her soul, until at last I no longer saw the dumb face of a donkey

---

24. gaidaros: (Modern) Greek for "ass."

25. Reference to Apuleius' ancient Roman novel *The Golden Ass* (late 2nd century A.D.) about a man accidentally transformed into an ass. After a long colorful journey he meets the goddess Isis who restores him.

when I looked upon her, but a sweet mind peering out through those deep brown eyes. I resolved to secretly transplant that brain into the hebetic body of her choice, but when I broached the subject she was horrified and professed to wanting no body other than the one she was born with. I vowed to accomplish this seemingly impossible task.

5 ACROSS THE FLOORS OF SEAS
LONG DEAD

There was a great deal of confusion in the aftermath of the raid. Benway was captured or fled for parts unknown, his mansion laboratory was in flames, and Linn and I were out on the streets of Lesser Freedonia[26] without a roof over our heads, nor any money. All we had, in fact, aside from my harness and short sword, were a few scalpels and a small pot of the copper-colored skin paint which, when applied to my pale skin, allowed me to pass as a red Jizmatic.

It seemed like an opportune time to set out for Mavrosia, but we needed provisions for such an arduous trek across the wastelands. Manual labor did not offer enough money, nor could I find any use for my new talents as surgeon since I knew nobody in the sprawling metropolis outside of the mansion. We soon hit upon a

---

26. Textual variation: In the *Interzone* text of "Under the Moons of Jizma," the term "Lesser Freedonia" is given as "lesser Annexia."

form of streetside theater,[27] playing upon Linn's unusual talents, and became minstrels for a few weeks until we had scraped[28] together enough money to outfit ourselves. And then we set out.

Although there was a great deal of hardship out on the desolate plains, those were perhaps the happiest of my days on Jizma. As we walked side by side, Linn told me of Jizma, its history and peoples, thus filling in my sketchy knowledge.

"Jizma has been settled by different races from different stars throughout the aeons. The first to arrive were the black-skinned Rmoahals,[29] who call themselves the 'First Born' of Jizma. Their place of origin is unknown, either lost to the sands of time or a secret guarded by death. Next came the golden Draconians and the pale Arians."

"Arians?" I asked, my blood warming.

"Yes, from Aries. When I first saw you, I supposed you might be one of them, returned from a nearly forgotten time, since they have been extinct for hundreds of thousands of years. Of course, now I believe your story, that you come from the planet Pyosis."[30]

"Tell me of the Arians," I pressed. "How did they come to die off?"

---

27. This theatrical act involving a talking ass alludes to the speaking sphincter from *Naked Lunch* (Ch. 16) section "the county clerk." Thus a meld of *The Golden Ass* and *Naked Lunch*.

28. Textual variation: In the *Interzone* text of "Under the Moons of Jizma," the term "scraped" is given as "scrapped."

29. Rmoahals: A subrace of the Atlantean root race in Madame Blavatsky's Theosophical writings.

30. Pyosis: Medical term for the forming or pouring out of pus. No clear connection to naming convention producing "Jizma."

"Legends say that they were not originally so ghost-like in complexion; they were more tan or brown. A terrible war was fought and lost, and the Arians were driven into deep caves while their continent was locked in an ice age. This was in that remote time before the oceans dried up.

"Deep in these caves, the Arians possessed so little food that they resorted to cannibalism, which is horror enough in itself, but in their case was even worse — since the first generation had been contaminated with *taqa,* or glowing-energy-poison, by eating this poisoned flesh they cursed themselves. They practiced unholy rites, as well, and developed strange new sorceries — including language. When at last they emerged from their ice-bound caves, they were pale from lack of sunlight and crazed from their poisons.[31] They conquered all of Jizma."

"Then what happened?"

"As a last-ditch effort, the First Born and the Draconians unleashed the dreaded *ak-karu,* green newtmen of Puuntango[32] [our Venus]. These terrible creatures killed indiscriminately, exterminating the Arians and driving all the others into the high-walled cities we still live in. The modern Jizmatic race of red men arose from the commingling of survivor races."

---

31. White race: In *Exterminator!* (1966) section "Astronaut Returns," WSB writes of an "ancient legend" that the white race resulted from an atomic explosion 30,000 years ago in what became the Gobi Desert; the radiation mutated the slaves into albinos. ERB's Mars has a white race that dominated the world in its wet phase but then fell into racial decline, such that in the dry phase the males are all bald and wear blond wigs—a detail that hauntingly anticipates hair loss due to radiation exposure.

32. Puuntango: Clearly a made-up word with no connection to the naming convention of "Jizma." The linkage of "green" to Venus is directly from WSB; for ERB, the green Martians are native to Mars and there are no Venusian humanoids present.

"How were the ak-karu halted?"

"The seas dried up," said Linn, flicking her head around to indicate the dry seabed around us. "The newt-men are amphibious and need water to birth their young. The adults are slower on land, so the fighting is more evenly matched."

"Are they oviparous, like the red men?" I asked.

"'Oviparous'? I suppose you could call the Jizmatic method something like that, since it does take place outside of the body. We usually call it *efevresis*."[33]

We ran out of food with one-third of the way left ahead of us. Linn was able to eke out some sustenance from the ocher lichen that was always underfoot, but I was starving. We took to resting during the heat of the day and traveling at night to conserve energy, but on the third such evening I fell and had a difficult time getting up again.

"Will, please ride me," said Linn. "Let me carry you."

"No, Linn," I mumbled. "I cannot do that."

"Oh 'Iron Will,' you must bend a little," Linn continued, butting my arm with her nose. "The packs are empty now, your weight would not be so great."

"But it would be so degrading for you, treating you like an animal . . . "

"Think of how often I have relied upon your arms. Now is the time to rely upon my legs to get us through this rough spot."

At last I relented and mounted the finest golden ass of Jizma, and then, having done so, I nearly shed a tear for Linn's incomparable spirit of self-sacrifice before I passed out from exhaustion.

---

33. efevresis: (Modern) Greek "invention."

6 PRISONERS OF THE GREEN JIZMATICS

The firearms of Jizma are wondrous marvels of advanced technology. Rather than having a metallic cartridge case, the bullet is embedded in a solid cake of propellant that is consumed when the bullet is fired. Reloading is quick and easy and since there is no ejection port, the weapon is completely sealed against the elements. The bullets themselves are of small caliber, making weapon recoil slight, but they are imbued with the explosive power of taqa, lending man-stopping power to a diminutive slug.

Thus, there was no contest when we found ourselves looking down the wrong end of a dozen rifles after quenching our thirst at an oasis. We surrendered to the newtmen. Linn and I were separated and the party moved off across the desert at a gallop toward a hill on the horizon.

It so happened that this hill had for its crown the ruins of an ancient seaport. As we neared the plaza of the dead city my presence was discovered and we were immediately surrounded by several dozen of the creatures, who seemed anxious to pluck me from my seat behind my guard. A word from the leader stilled their clamor and we proceeded at a trot across the plaza to the entrance of a palace that was magnificent even in death.

The edifice was low but covered an enormous area. It was constructed of white marble inlaid with gold and brilliant stones that sparkled in the sunlight. The entrance was some hundred feet in width, and a gentle incline to the second floor opened onto an enormous chamber encircled by galleries. On the floor of this chamber were assembled about forty or fifty male green Jizmatics around the steps of a dais covered with Aztec mosaics. Murals indicated that this once proud city had been built by the ancient Arians, yet now it was merely a temporary shelter for nomadic tribes and the air was cloyed with a sweet evil substance like decayed honey.

On the platform itself squatted an enormous green warrior festooned with metal ornaments, gay-colored feathers and beautifully wrought leather trappings. His lips were thin and purple-blue, slightly beaked like that of a snapping turtle, and his eyes were blank with insect calm. From his shoulders hung a short cape of white fur lined with brilliant scarlet silk.

The ideas of humor among the green men of Jizma are widely at variance with our concepts, as I was about to learn. The death agonies of a comrade are, to these strange creatures, cause of the wildest hilarity, while their main form of amusement is to inflict death upon their prisoners of war in various ingenious and horrible ways. Their laughter signifies torture, suffering, and death.

A guard brought out a pale white boy, the sight of which caused a surge of recognition throughout the chamber — an age-long racial hatred among the green men, whereas I felt a sense of kinship for the lad. The leader tied the boy's hands behind him with a red silk cord. An assistant parted the silk curtains, revealing a gallows on the dais, and the leader propelled the Arian boy up the steps and under the noose.

The boy struggled valiantly but was easily subdued by the green man who towered nearly four feet over him. The leader slipped the noose over the boy's head and tightened the knot. The boy looked straight ahead, breathing deeply. The green Jizmatic began striking at the boy's back with his tail, lightly at first, but then flailing savagely until it seemed that the lad would faint and strangle himself. Then, tired of playing, the laughing tormentor reached down and snapped the boy's neck, and at this grisly climax the members of his inner circle moved in to feed upon the victim's essence.[34]

The horror! The horror![35]

I looked away from this ghoulish feast and realized with sickening dread that I would be next in the afternoon's entertainment. I wheeled around with my back to the nearest pillar, expecting to be overwhelmed but determined to give them as good a battle as the unequal odds would permit before I gave up my life.

Things were at their grimmest. Linn was at my side, protecting my flank with bone-breaking kicks, while I emptied the magazines of every pistol I could lay hand to with deadly accuracy, and though the bodies piled up around us, still they kept coming. Then, suddenly, a series of terrific explosions sounded outside, and before long a hundred ebony-skinned warriors flowed into the palace, cutting down the awful green men in their wake with sword-and-gun play. When they caught sight of the hanged boy, their fighting took on a new fury.

---

34. This sequence, from Aztec mosaic through red silk bindings to hanging, seems drawn from *Naked Lunch* (Ch. 9) section "hassan's rumpus room."

35. The horror: Allusion to Conrad's *Heart of Darkness* (section III), where these are the last words of Kurtz, the chief of the Inner Station.

Within minutes the massacre was over. As a group of the victors moved to cut down the boy and others began the looting of the dead, their commander shouted over to us, "You there! Who are you? Friend of the newtmen or foe?"

"Foe," I answered, advancing slowly with my hands up. "I was next in line for the gallows, I am afraid."

"Hold," he said. "You wear the trappings of Freedonia."

"We are simple entertainers from Annexia," I explained.

"'We'?" he asked, looking around for other red men.

"This gaidaros and I," I said. "We were travelling to a distant place and were captured on our way by these monsters. Thank you for saving us."

"But we are at war with Freedonia," he said, drawing his pistol. "So you are our prisoner. Or prisoners. You can save your stories for the Empress."

At this point, Linn spoke up. "Iron Will, meet Steelie Dan,[36] Lord Captain of the Black Pirates of Jizma. Steelie Dan, meet Iron Will, the man from Pyosis."

---

36. Steelie Dan: Perhaps the most famous name from *Naked Lunch* is Steely Dan, found in (Ch. 11) section "a.j.'s annual party."

7 QUEEN OF LIFE AND DEATH

The pirates took us aboard their fantastic airboats[37] that operated by a cosmic force unknown to Earth science. The landscape below raced by in excess of two hundred miles per hour as my savior-captors forced me to remove the remaining red paint from my skin. Dawn found us descending over the ruins of Koreh, a vast city in a broad mountain valley across the equator and nearly halfway around the world from Freedonia. It offered a sight both imposing and melancholic — mile after mile of toppled columns, demolished temples, and crumbling palaces scattered throughout the green of a lush vegetation that seemed out of place on this arid world.

But it was not entirely abandoned. The ships quickly landed and I was escorted into a temple where, standing before a burnished throne that shone like beaten gold,[38] stood a glorious and regal figure. I must have become

---

37. Textual variation: previously "airships."

38. Phrases "burnished throne" and "beaten gold" seem drawn from Shakespeare's *Antony and Cleopatra* (Act II, ii).

overly accustomed to the adolescent physiques of Jizmatic women in my several months on their world, for the sight of a full-figured woman struck me literally dumb with wonder.

Her long thick hair fell in dark tapering ringlets on her lovely white neck. Just above her brow shone a round disk. Her many-colored robe was of fine linen; part was white, part yellow, part red. But what caught and held my eye more than anything else was the deep black luster of her mantle, slung from shoulder to hip, and embroidered with glittering stars on the hem.[39]

"My Queen," said Steelie Dan, bowing low. "Prince Kerz, he is dead."[40]

With a low moan Ayssa sat down upon the throne. I was torn by a storm of conflicting emotions. This creature was more than a queen: she was a goddess incarnate. But what of Linn? The base impulses of my heart were grappling with the more noble aspirations of my mind.

"All is not lost," continued Steelie Dan. "We brought his body back. And by strange chance and coincidence we captured a white madman who wears the harness of Freedonia yet claims to be from Pyosis."

I stepped forward, but before I could utter a salutation her blue eyes flashed with fire and she bolted upright.

"You!" she cried. "Marcus!"

"O Queen Ayssa, I am William Lee of Earth, third planet from the sun," I said, suddenly finding my tongue. "I set out from Lesser Freedonia in the company of Linn the talking ass with the single purpose of journeying to

---

39. Her wardrobe is like that of Isis in *The Golden Ass*, chapter 47.

40. Allusion to Conrad's *Heart of Darkness*, where Kurtz was the chief of the Inner Station. Famous line from section III: "Mistah Kurtz—he dead."

your court in order to beg you to show mercy upon your subject and return Linn's brain to its previous body."

Her gaze cooled considerably. "So, the proud Polluxian is behind this? Is Linn here? Bring the beast at once!" Then she turned to me again. "Why is your skin so pale? Are you a Polluxian like Linn? Or perhaps a Spician?"

"No, my Queen," I said. "I am a Virginian, from Pyosis."

"A Virgoan colony on Pyosis?" she said, arching an eyebrow. "What a novel thought. Perhaps you are mad."[41]

---

41. Ayssa is obviously based on Ayesha [pronounced "Assah"], a.k.a. She-who-must-be-obeyed, the subject of *She* (1887) by H. Rider Haggard. Ayesha is the white queen of a black tribe; she rules from the ruins of Kôr, a lost city of Africa; she recognizes in Leo, the hero's young charge, a reincarnation of her lover from ancient Greece. There is also a thread from ERB's Martian novel *Llana of Gathol* (1948), where a group of black Martians reside in the Valley of the First Born in the tropics north of the equator. In this fashion, Steelie Dan matches Doxus, jeddak of the Black Pirates of Kamtol.

8 AYSSA UNVEILED

Once we were alone in her private chambers, Ayssa turned to me and said, "How are things in Rome these days?" It was another shock, since she had spoken to me in Latin!

I answered in kind, saying, "I know not, my Queen, since Rome lies far to the east of my country, across the ocean."

"Ah, so you come from the Hesperides," she said in Greek, smiling. "And how fares the mighty Republic? How prospers the family of Caesar?"

"The family of Caesar is long extinct, O Queen," I responded, struggling to keep up.

"And his Republic?"

"Long faded, O Queen."

"How long ago?" she asked in the Jizmatic tongue. "Of what year is the city? I would guess it to be nearly nine hundred and forty years of age."

"I know not the age of Rome, my Queen," I said. "But nearly two millennia have passed since the death of Caesar."

"You lie!" she shouted.

"No, mighty Queen."

"Heed me, mortal," she said. "I will not be toyed with.

If this be some elaborate jape, your fate is sealed with a death undreamt by the newtmen. Your miserable, worthless life hangs by the slenderest of threads. Now tell me the whole of your life and adventure, I command it!"

Cast in a role like that of Scheherazade,[42] but compelled to truth rather than fabrication, I told of the adventures and misadventures which had led me from my ancestral home of Virginia through the jungles of the Amazon to my advent upon Mars.

"You materialized in a public lavatory?" she asked.[43]

"Yes, O Queen," I answered. "At the Pneumatic Tube Station of Greater Freedonia."

"Continue," she commanded.

I told of my apprenticeship under Benway, Master Mind of Jizma, which abruptly terminated with the raid by the Health Police, then of my desert trek with Linn.

"You seem rather fond of Linn," said Ayssa.

"I am," I declared. "Linn has been my best and truest friend on Jizma."

"Might your feelings for Linn be described as love?"

"Yes, they might," I said, feeling anew that tangle of emotions.

"Do you think Linn more beautiful than I?" she said, arching her back slightly.

"No," I stammered. "Of course not, O Queen. You are more beautiful than anyone."

"Perhaps you only say that because I hold your life in

---

42. Scheherazade: the central storyteller of *One Thousand and One Nights*. Briefly, the sultan, enraged at discovering his wife an adultress, resolved to marry a new virgin every day and behead the wife of the day before. Scheherazade was virgin wife number 1,001, and she told the stories to prolong her life.

43. public lavatory: In *Naked Lunch* (Ch. 7) section "hospital," WSB's Benway uses a locked lavatory as an operating room.

my hand," she said softly with a wan smile. "Continue with your account."

I did so. As I finished, who should be escorted into the chamber but Benway himself, summoned by way of wireless telephony and transported by swift airboat. He immediately prostrated himself upon the floor and cried, "Hail Empress Ayssa, Queen of Life and Death! This slave is yours to dispose of."

"Arise, Benway," she said. "Behold this man — do you know him?"

The Master Mind turned to me and his docile expression gave way to the astonishment of recognition. "You!" he ejaculated. "Will Gigim! Are you truly a ghost this time?"

"Silence, Will," said Ayssa. "Doctor, answer the question."

Benway corroborated my story as I stood by in silence.

"Explain the raid," she said.

"Either the Health and Hygiene League or Security Troops from the Ministry of Health. Whichever one, the hand of Pretender Koyotel is behind it."

"Koyotel!" she cursed. "We should have killed her long ago. How is her power?"

"She now controls the Ministries of Health and Labor and seems to have succeeded in bending the ear of her husband the King. I fear an expedition fleet is being assembled against us."

"Why did you not tell me this before?" demanded Ayssa. "Why did you not bring this man Will to me immediately?"

"A thousand excuses leap to my tongue," said Benway after a pause. "But none of them dare to face thee, O Queen. Kill me now, if you wish."

"I hope that your skills as scientist will be more useful than your skills as spy. I charge you to your workshop to create the armies of synthetic men[44] you have promised me. With them we may be able to fend off the Freedonian attack. Without them we are doomed. Go."

"Yes, O Queen," said Benway, prostrating himself again. "With the assistance of Will I can achieve this goal in half the time . . . "

"I will send him soon — now go!"

Once we were alone again, Ayssa turned to me. "Will, I am impressed with your story. There are some details which yet puzzle me, but there are many things you have spoken of which are unknown to the people of Jizma. I, too, am from Earth, but this is a closely guarded secret. You must swear to tell no one!"

I swore upon my honor, and then she sketched for me her own fantastic adventure, of how she had died in a manner similar to me (in her case, the bite of an aquatic centipede) and had awoken among the ruins of Koreh. The black pirates using the area as their base witnessed her materialization, and they had readily accepted her as a goddess.

"You have called me beautiful, such as men have named me on both worlds," she said. "But I have not changed a bit since the day I woke up here, and that was some two hundred and thirteen years ago!"

---

44. synthetic men: Referencing ERB novel *Synthetic Men of Mars* (1940), ninth in the Mars series, in which previously introduced Master Mind of Mars, Ras Thavas, begins producing factory-made vat-grown humanoids.

9 A RACE AGAINST TIME

Linn's surgical transfer was preceded by a simple yet curious ceremony of atonement. In a large assembly hall filled with the few hundred of her subjects, Ayssa held out a single red rose. Linn approached slowly, bowed deeply, and then ate the rose from her hand.[45] Benway led Linn away for the operation and I went back to work on the vats.

Several hours later I stumbled into the Queen's dining chamber by previous appointment. Ayssa, Benway, and Steelie Dan were already seated. I apologized for being late.

"How did the surgery go?" I asked Benway as one of Ayssa's half-dozen or so white princes acted as server.

"Well, very well," Benway answered. "But what of your work?"

"It progresses, but slowly." We then launched into a technical discussion of growing tissue in vat cultures, a conversation that lasted for most of the meal. I had

45. ate the rose: Alluding to ceremony with Ass and Isis in *The Golden Ass,* chapter 47.

noticed the lad attending us kept trying to make eye contact with me, and I was getting slightly annoyed at him. As the scientific talk died down, I returned to the previous subject.

"So tell me, doctor, how is the patient? I am surprised that Linn did not join us for supper."

"Ah, but Linn did join us," said the Master Mind, a laugh on his lips. With a sweep of his hand he indicated our waiter. "Iron Will, meet Prince Linn of the Polluxi. Prince Linn, meet Iron Will of Pyosis."

No doubt my face showed some fraction of the surprise and horror I felt. The others began laughing loudly, and Linn fled the room in shame.

"What . . . have you done?" I finally managed to blurt out.

"Exactly what you asked me to do — I returned Linn's brain to his original body. Do you not like him? Is he not a fine specimen?"

"O my Will, what visions I have seen!" cried Ayssa. "Methought you were enamored of an ass."[46] She redoubled her laughter.

Suddenly my crisis of rage and confusion dissolved in catharsis; and realizing that my feelings for Linn had always been those of comradeship or brotherly love rather than any other kind, I laughed along with them.

My heart and mind were now drawn to one object, the peerless Ayssa, and by some strange magic, she too was drawn to me. I vowed to be her slave and she offered me marriage instead, speaking of how we would found a new race on Jizma, the Fifth Race of prophecy.

"A virile race of kings," she murmured when we were

---

46. Ayssa reshapes a line from near the end of Shakespeare's *A Midsummer Night's Dream,* where the Fairy Queen Titania says to her husband, "My Oberon, what visions have I seen! Methought I was enamored of an ass." (Act IV, i)

back in her private chambers after the ceremony. "We will sweep clean this decadent planet, uniting all under our banner. We will shun *efevresis* in favor of our old Earth magic. Let the subject races hatch and decant their pathetic offspring; ours will be born.

"You see, Will, this has been my secret, I am the only real woman on this world. Do you understand? They have forgotten, in their racial senility. We have that which they lack. Jizma is a no-man's world, and I have been so lonely, ever so lonely without you, but now you are here."

"Yes, my Ayssa."

"'Ayssa' is just a title," she said. "When we are alone together, you may call me Thea, since that is my name. Now look, Will, see here the sign of our new race." She drew a circle with a cross inside. "By this sign shall we conquer Jizma with Earth magic . . ."

10 THE PILLAR OF LIGHT

Having never been in battle before, I have difficulty expressing the horror and confusion that met us on the morning when the attack finally came. By the time I arrived on the scene, several of our pirate vessels lay destroyed on the ground, while the others had either fled or were fighting beyond the valley wall. Drifting across the sky was a fearsome armada flying the crossed hammer-and-sword of Freedonia, slowly moving in for the kill. Explosive projectiles were going off all around, from the sharp cracks of the small arms up through to the thunderous blasts of heavy ordnance.

Since even our rifles were useless against the ship hulls, Linn and I were desperately trying to prevent ships from landing and discharging troops by waiting until they came in close and then spraying the decks with rapid fire. Nearby, our only heavy gun emplacement was valiantly hammering away at the Freedonian ships with one-inch-diameter bullets. A stream of these potent projectiles managed to tear a gash in the buoyancy tank of a ship maneuvering to land, and it plummeted into the tangle of jungle-covered ruins. The crew of another enemy ship struggled to extinguish a deck fire while Linn and I tried to keep them from succeeding.

A few pirate vessels swooped into view from the west, giving us hope, but then our heavy gun fell suddenly silent. The gunner had been killed, but the gun itself appeared to be operable, and since it was all that we had, I ran over to man it myself.

I never got there. Instead I ran into what I can only describe as a pillar of light.

There was pain, a great deal of pain. My life flashed before my eyes, the past, the present, and even the future . . .

". . . in the interests of science, to measure the crania of those going out there . . ."

A game of Jizmatic chess, red against white, where pieces can turncoat unexpectedly . . .

Koyotel snarled, "Die, Conquistador! Die!" . . .

. . . Jizma is only the outer plain, threshold to the astral plain . . .

Ayssa held out a single red rose . . .

"What, are you some kind of *gigim*? A ghost . . ."

Finally, the whiteness became so white that it was black.

---

47. In Haggard's *She*, the Pillar of Fire is a portal to immortality or death.

11 THE EMBRACE OF DEATH

It was dawn when I opened my eyes again, awakened by the sound of my own death rattle. My mouth was full of dust and strange, stiff garments were upon my body; garments that cracked into powder as I rose to a sitting posture.

As I comprehended the dried-out corpse on the couch beside me I realized that I was back in the cave of Lupita. My death on Jizma had sent me back to Earth! But I was as weak as a newborn babe. It took all of my energy and a good part of the morning to crawl across the cave to where the bundles of wild honey sat, offerings to savage gods unnamed. As I reached for the honey, I saw my own hand for the first time and was horrified to see its boney and semi-desiccated appearance. I had somehow been mummified!

I will not bore you with the details of my return to civilization. Suffice to say, after gorging myself upon honey and rainwater for three days, I emerged from the cave and made my way north. When I arrived at the town of Manaós I found it greatly expanded, more than I thought possible in the year or so I had been away. Dr. Monygham was nowhere to be found. Then I learned that the year was

1896, and fully nine years had passed since I had set out into the jungle.

With the financial assistance of missionaries and scientists I returned to my homeland. If strangers had difficulty accepting my story, that was nothing compared to friends and family. They were by turns shocked, horrified, skeptical, and sympathetic. Gradually they came to believe in my identity, if not in my whereabouts for the last decade.

I discovered that Mr. Bradly Martin, my employer, had married my widowed mother within a few months of my departure, thinking that I would soon return from what he thought was a wild goose chase and grow to accept his new status in the house as a *fait accompli*. As for my old college chum Teddy, he is still living in New York City, now as head of the police board, but he is gravitating towards Washington D.C. again, having served there for a few years during my absence. Telling him of my adventure rekindled the old fires, and he talked of organizing expeditions, though I sensed even he only halfheartedly believed me.

But that is no matter, since I know what I know. Thanks to Benway's advanced science, I have created a new painkiller, more powerful than morphine yet lacking its addictive properties. I call it "Ayssa" after the person I consider the real heroine of this adventure, my wife and queen on another world. In addition, we have a secret ingredient for a new soft drink — Mr. Bradly Martin's prediction has proven remarkably accurate, as witnessed by the rise of the Anti-Saloon League in Ohio. A Mr. Asa Candler bought the secret of Coca-Cola for the princely sum of two thousand three hundred dollars. Clearly Pemberton thinks[48] it has topped out, but we are willing to

---

48. Pemberton thinks: John Pemberton, Coke inventor, died in 1888; his son and heir, Charley Pemberton, died in 1894. William Lee was out of the country during that time, but even so, his

bet that Candler will go far and we intend to catch or surpass him. Look out, Coke, here comes "Jazmine!"

It seems that Madame Sosostris died in the same year that Candler made his purchase.[49] But I wonder if that was the last we will see of her. For in searching for a new chemical compound, it seems that I have stumbled upon a Fountain of Youth, if not Immortality itself.

You might laugh at such a claim coming from this withered body. My own experience proves that time passes more swiftly on Earth than on Jizma, at a ratio of roughly nine to one. Whole vistas of ancient and forgotten science have opened up for me. I now know the secrets of the Pharaohs, and why honey was placed in their tombs for their eventual return. Consider Ayssa, with her Jizmatic century of incomparable beauty, and how nineteen centuries have passed on Earth in that period. I have learned her identity on Earth — she is none other than Thea Philopator, better known as Cleopatra — and I plan to re-enter Jizma from Alexandria, Egypt, in order to arrive at the ruined city of Koreh. But I must hurry. Even now the battle rages. Though I have time dilation on my side, still every second counts. Has the red queen Koyotel yet succeeded in killing my white queen Ayssa? Has brave Linn fallen in battle or been taken prisoner? Has Benway completed the army of synthetic men? I find that liberal

---

thoughts seem scattered here.

49. Sosostris and the Coca-Cola purchase: Madame Blavatsky, one possible candidate for T.S. Eliot's "Sosostris," died in 1891. (There is continuing controversy regarding the possible influence of Blavatsky's Theosophical texts upon ERB's Mars series.) The transfer of Coca-Cola involved some complications of its own: while Asa Candler bought a majority of the company in 1888, he certainly gained control of Coca-Cola in 1891. William Lee's thoughts here might be scattered, or it might be "fog of war."

use of cocaine allows me to complete more work within the brief hours of a day, but I must return to Jizma as quickly as possible.

The red planet is calling me: Mars, the god of war, but his more ancient title is the flayed god, He-who-is-sacrificed. Jizma summons me, a call I cannot resist. Ayssa beckons me, and it is She-who-must-be-obeyed.

The Gods of Jizma[50]

---

50. Clearly an allusion to ERB's second Mars novel, *The Gods of Mars* (serialized 1913). The "sequel" to *Naked Lunch* is WSB's *The Soft Machine* (1961), first novel of the Nova Trilogy.

INTRODUCTION (1913) BY NORMAN
LEE BEAN[51]

In sharing the strange tale of my uncle's astral travel to the
weird world of Jizma in 1887, his return to Earth in 1896,
and his setting out in 1897 to search our globe for another
portal to the red planet — in doing that, I inadvertently
infected my readers with the same questions that I alone
had heretofore pondered for a dozen years: Did Dr. Lee in
fact find a portal in Egypt, or did he meet misfortune and
die anonymously in the desert sands?

What about Ayssa, the woman known on Earth as
Cleopatra? At the very moment William Lee abruptly
translated back to Earth, Ayssa's city-state was under
attack by an aerial navy. What was her fate, and that of
Lee's gay companion Linn? And what of Dr. Benway, the
Master Mind of Jizma who first befriended Lee? In short,
the world cries out: "What happened next?"

---

51. Norman Lee Bean: Here it is revealed that the nephew of
William Lee has a middle name of "Lee." Clearly Norman's
mother was born a "Lee."

I have received many letters asking such questions, but there was also one missive that was quite different: a famous scientist who believes he has received wireless transmissions[52] from Jizma, transmissions from Dr. Lee himself. This scientist (whom I will refer to as "N.T.")[53] was performing experiments with the Hertzian Wave around the turn of the century, when he chanced to hear a human voice. N.T. recorded the voice on a wax cylinder gramophone. More than one cylinder, in fact, on more than one occasion. Over a period of nights the voice spoke, telling an incredible tale of adventures on Jizma. Some parts were repeated, yet there seem to be gaps in the narrative. Still, it begins with Dr. Lee in Alexandria, Egypt, and ends with his broadcast from the perverse paradise of Jizma.

---

52. wireless transmissions: For ERB novels, a fictitious "Gridley wave" allowed ERB to contact first Pellucidar in *Tanar of Pellucidar* (1929 serial), then Mars for *A Fighting Man of Mars* (1930 serial) and *Synthetic Men of Mars* (1939 serial).

53. N.T.: Patently a reference to Nikola Tesla (1856–1943). In 1899 Tesla reported unusual signals from his radio receiver and speculated they might come from another planet.

1 VOICE FROM THE ETHER

Jizma to Earth, Jizma to Earth — this is Lee reporting. We have taken the Dream Palace, I repeat, we have taken the Dream Palace. After so much fighting we will take a short rest before beginning our assault on the Reality Laboratory. I am using this time to tell everything of my return to Jizma.

I remember the beginning like a dream. On the Mediterranean Sea the ship drew near to Egypt, and out of the mellowest of sunsets I saw the domes and minarets of Alexandria rise into view. Once onto the pier, I had to press through the army of Egyptian boys with their tiny donkeys, waiting for passengers. Throwing caution to the wind, I rode one in a furious gallop, driven by boys running behind, to the hotel.

After securing a room, I began my exploration, finding a city of huge commercial buildings served by broad, handsome streets brilliant with gaslight — all swarming with swarthy Egyptians, dark Turks, and black Abyssinians, I might add. But Alexandria was too much like a European city. By night it was a blurry mirage of Paris;[54] by

_____

54. These paragraphs seem drawn from Mark Twain's visit to

47

day it was the vision that inspired Marc Antony's trans-formation of Rome from brick into marble.[55]

Round and round through this labyrinth I went, search-ing for a way to find the hidden tomb of Cleopatra. Her famed temple was drowned long ago, of course. The next best place is Taposiris Magna over at Abusir, about forty miles southwest along the coast. But I needed a guide. I searched from high to low — from the embassy, to the adventurers' club, to a seance parlor, to a hashish den. All I got was a thin lead on The Kid.

I found the ice cream parlor,[56] and therein found my guide The Kid.

He was young. He had a weird look to his eyes. People had said he was epileptic.[57]

I asked him if he spoke English.

He said, "Ice cream."

I bought him a bowl of the stuff. As he ate he became progressively more coherent, in the manner of a drunk sobering up with coffee. We spoke of my need to find the place. He gave me his conditions, and I hired him. I took him back to my hotel room to keep him close.

We went down the coast toward Libya, to the shores of Mariut — it is a lake separated from the sea by a narrow

---

Alexandria in *The Innocents Abroad* (1869), Ch. LVII.

55. Marc Antony: Contrary to the text, it was Augustus who claimed "I found Rome a city of bricks and left it a city of marble" rather than Marc Antony. Then again, Marc spent more time in Alexandria.

56. Alexandrian ice cream parlor: Twain mentions such a place, calling it an "ice-cream saloon."

57. epileptic: This links to the boy guide in WSB's *The Soft Machine* (Ch. 2) section "Who Am I to Be Critical?"

ridge of land. Atop this ridge squats the local acropolis. That is Taposiris Magna. An outcropping of limestone surrounded at its base by palm trees, with its top adorned by the ruins of a lighthouse and a few temples. One temple was dedicated to Osiris, Egyptian god of the afterlife. Another temple was for his wife Isis.

Now, The Kid was like a dowsing rod, or a bloodhound for ghosts. I allowed him to handle the ring of Cleopatra and her comb, which gave him the scent. He started casting around but came up empty. We marched over that limestone from end to end. I bribed, I threatened, I begged. Nothing.

We returned to Alexandria and tried sensing her in the water over her drowned temple. No luck, which was just as well since I could not see how I was going to work underwater. Still, it was a tough spot, with no leads to follow. We grew desperate and began casting around at places in the city, always at night. At one point I had The Kid so stuffed with ice cream that his lips were turning blue, and we went out for what I had decided would be the last time.

We walked for miles. He could sense that our time was at an end, and he wept with regret on top of frustration. We were down at the marina again when he tried something new, putting the ring and comb in his mouth. Straight away we moved inland, and after a few blocks he stiffened, jerked around, and went into a pitch-black alley.

I will not be more specific. We went through a tunnel. The Kid led me to the secret tomb of Cleopatra. Unfortunately he blundered into a trap that killed him.[58] The mummy of Cleopatra was there, along with necessary reagents. I stocked the tomb with bottles of water and bags of sugar for our eventual return, then I cooked up a

---

58. a trap that killed him: The epileptic boy guide in "Who Am I to Be Critical?" also dies to permit travel between worlds.

dose of the strange elixir and shot my essence across the ether back to Jizma.[59]

---

59. This action, wherein the protagonist lies down by his beloved's side in her tomb by the sea, finds echo with Edgar Allan Poe's posthumous poem "Annabel Lee" (1849).

2 RETURN TO JIZMA

Dr. William Lee found himself in darkness, lying upon a hard surface. The air was close and still, giving him a creeping dread that he had been buried alive.

Reaching for matches in his pocket, he discovered he was naked. He shouted for joy, seeing this as proof he had transmitted to Jizma. His voice echoed back immediately from nearby walls and ceiling.

He crawled around, feeling for pit and wall. The surface seemed to be marble. He found a wall and followed it to the right. He found another wall, and this one had a heavy door.

Lee pushed it open and emerged into the late afternoon at Koreh, city of Ayssa. The door locked as it closed behind him, sealing the shrine to Ayssa's transmission.

He was in the palace garden. The garden was in a disarray of neglect and ill use, causing his surging heart to falter. When he saw the flag of Freedonia flying at the palace, his blood ran cold.

He heard voices of men off to the right. He went to the left, searching for clothing. He found a gardener's shed and quickly fashioned himself an apron with a length of rope and a scrap of canvas. This done, he searched for other possible tools or weapons, but there was only a surveyor's tripod. He unbolted its outsized telescope and climbed up onto the roof to reconnoiter the area.

The group of men were red, presumably occupation soldiers in this city of blacks. They were engaged in rooster combat.

The Jizmatic rooster[60] has one eye, like a Cyclops, and is used in a gambling blood sport. The fighting takes place in an oval nine feet by seven, marked by three chalk lines in the middle, a long one with two short ones parallel to it three feet away.

Lee turned his attention to the palace, looking for clues. A white figure came around the side, a youth bearing a rooster in a cage. Lee felt a jolt of surprise, recognizing his young friend Linn, but then he felt concern.

Linn sauntered over to the oval, where the soldiers greeted him with familiarity. This perplexed Lee; could the soldiers be mercenaries loyal to Ayssa? Not with the flag of Freedonia flying!

Lee wanted to meet with Linn, but Linn alone. As Linn entered the oval, all eyes were focused there, so Lee got down from the shed and made his way in the gathering dusk to the side-yard Linn had come through. Here he hid himself and peered through the telescope while waiting for Linn to return the way he had come.

Linn was still in the oval. Lee saw the roosters fly up and strike down with spurs. The handlers separated them when they got stuck.

Then it was over and Linn was the victor. Another fight was agreed to. After all the bets were made, the handlers primed the birds by thrusting the roosters together to enrage them. When they put them down behind the short lines, the fight started.

Linn emerged triumphant again. He put his rooster

---

60. rooster: A link to *The Ticket That Exploded* (Ch. 3 and 8).

back in its cage, collected all his winnings, and started walking toward Lee's pathway. One soldier detached from the rest and hurried to catch up, then walk with Linn. The soldier was trying to convince Linn of something, but Linn was cheerfully refusing. As they came closer, Lee could make out the words.

"Listen," said the soldier, "you've had a good run with your bird, but it can't go on much longer. Everybody around here knows he's the best, so your winnings won't be as good as when you started. Sell him to me now for top price."

"No, thank you."

The soldier grabbed him by the arm.

"Look, boy, you ain't in a position —"

Lee halted his threat by knocking him unconscious with the telescope.

Linn recognized Lee in an instant, and together they quietly fled the palace grounds.

At the first opportunity, Lee asked about Ayssa.

"Ever since you disappeared, Queen Ayssa has grieved and mourned. Did not all Koreh suffer the loss of her lord? Certes! But none more than she. Our beloved queen drooped lower and lower, until it was plain to all that it were only a matter of days ere she went to end her sorrows within the fields of Gazma.

"So there was but little surprise when one day she was gone. No word left she, but it is always thus with those who go upon the voluntary pilgrimage from which none returns."

"Wait," cried Lee. "Is she dead?"

"No," said Linn. "She has gone up the Return Canal to Gazma."[61]

---

61. Her pilgrimage: This plot point mirrors one in *The Gods of Mars* but there it comes late in the novel (chapter 18, out of twenty-two chapters), rather than early.

"What, pray tell, is this *Gazma* of which you speak?"

"Only the land of love and peace and rest to which every Jizmatic since time immemorial has longed to pilgrimage at the end of a life of hate and strife and bloodshed."

"How long has it been since she left? Might we yet catch up with her on this side of Gazma?"[62]

"Yes, but only if we fly as quickly as possible."

---

62. Gazma: An Arabic word with many meanings, including "shoe," "stupid girl," and "dirt." How any of this could relate to "Paradise" remains obscure. Perhaps only selected because it sounds so close to "Jizma."

3 UP THE SACRED CANAL OF JIZMA

Now, on Jizma the southern hemisphere is all uphill. I know, I know — it sounds impossible. I found it hard to believe, too, until I saw it myself. It seems so unnatural, violating the symmetry we take for granted, but at the same time it permits the canal system to function. That is, five canals allow water to flow from the South Polar region to the rest of a desert planet. There is also the one canal that draws water back to the South Pole, and this is the Holy Canal of Return.[63]

At this point in my palaver, a listener might reasonably be asking, "So water flows *uphill* on Jizma?" No, it does not. Remember, these are canals, artificial constructs. The water is continually pumped up against the gradient and prevented from flowing away again by a chain of locks. The total rise must be a couple of miles at least. The pumps are primitive and durable, powered by treadmills

---

63. Canals of Mars: Maps by the astronomer Percival Lowell (1855–1916) play a big part in ERB's vision of Mars. For example, it seems likely that ERB's "Helium" is based on "Hellas" on the maps of canals.

walked upon by slaves, convicts, and pilgrims — pilgrims who piously pay for the privilege.

One must picture a canal work to lift seawater up to Boulder Colorado, a bigger project than that French dream of a cut across Panama. It rises up, a stairway of pumps and reservoirs, until it gets to Argyre and dives underground at the south end, to emerge eventually in Gazma, the Eden of Jizma, somewhere near the South Pole.[64]

I have told it badly to give the context. In fact I did not see a problem or care about the details, since I assumed that an airboat could carry us to Gazma at two hundred miles per hour. My companions explained to me that the lifting power diminishes with altitude, such that the airboats could only go halfway up the Pilgrim Rise. So our itinerary was to fly to Ladon Reservoir, then make our way up the Uzboi Water to Argyre.[65] At each place we would look for Ayssa.

Steelie Dan, that great black pirate captain, flew us over there in his airboat. If I had known what was ahead I would have quit at that point.

So Linn and I arrived at Ladon, a body of water that must be two hundred miles long, with pumps at either end and a city on both shores. This is halfway up the Pilgrim Rise.

Now, at that time I was largely innocent of Jizmatic religion. There had been no regular temples in Ayssa's city Koreh, and while I had seen several in Freedonia and Annexia, I had never been inside one.

That changed. This being the holy land, there were temples everywhere, sometimes one next to another. After

---

64. Earthly paradise at south pole: Gazma matches ERB's "Valley Dor," believed to be the Barsoomian Heaven itself.

65. Ladon, Uzboi, Argyre: Three real Martian locations, named by astronomers succeeding Lowell.

we spent an exhausting day questioning the countermen of hotels, inns, and hostels, searching for Ayssa, we visited a temple. Temples on Jizma seem to be open for worship from around midday to midnight. In some ways it is like church — for example, services last two hours or more — but collection is taken at the door.

One enters the place, a big room, cavernous, and it is lit by radium bulbs. The ceiling is high, ornate with designs, but there are no stained glass windows — no windows at all. There are the pews, and down at the front there is a short run of steps up to a stage, with a pulpit off to the left and a giant curtain on the back wall. I figured that curtain hid the holiest of holies.

A priest comes down the aisle, mounts the steps, spreads his arms wide and calls everyone to worship. The talking dies down, all stand up, and sing through a song. Then two boys on the stage pull the curtains aside to reveal a vast black wall, maybe thirty feet high, and not a mark on it.

But then something happens, something I find hard to express in words. There is a moment of color in the middle of the wall, and then it expands into an image of a beautiful place, an Eden, so it is like a window onto this paradise, but everything is giant-sized. Then the images move — I mean, there are these giants who walk and talk, and they look like normal people except they are gigantic, so that, for instance, that apple she is holding must be the size of a hut. So it is like a play by giants, done with light like an elaborate magic lantern show. Then the people get bigger and smaller, changing all the time, so it is not like a play, just like it was not like a window, and yet it is like a window and a play and a magic lantern show. They call these "flickers."[66]

---

66. flickers: In *The Gods of Mars* ERB has the Martian religion of Issus and the pilgrimage to the Martian Heaven, but he never describes a normal church service or the ways of pilgrims. WSB

I got used to it — seems we went nearly every evening, so I learned. But then my understanding was overturned one night at a temple up in Uzboi.

It happened during one of the short pieces before the sermon, this time being something called "Hello from Heaven," showing all these bright and shining pilgrims who had just stepped off their rafts, arriving at Gazma. Most of them were red, with a scattering of blacks and yellows, but my eye was caught by the sight of a white woman — it was Ayssa!

Well, when I saw that I shouted and stood up, because everything was ruined — there was the woman I had crossed the ether for, snatched away from me! I ran down the pew, then down the aisle, crying out to her. The priest and the curtain boys tried to stop me, but I shook them off and mounted the stage where I pounded on the strange wall of images.

One of those images took notice of me. He was standing like a statue holding up the talking woman's desk, one of many statues, just a decoration. But he looked down at me and then he came forward out of the wall. Silvery marble sort of color, he was, and man-sized. He took my shoulder — I felt it, real as can be — and he said, "You will meet her again in Gazma, pilgrim."

He walked me back to my pew, then he walked back to the stage, where he stepped up into the wall again.

That was my first flickerman.

I must admit my teeth were chattering. It was like I had seen a ghost, or an angel. Later Tilly shot one, and it turned to silver smoke in a moment, which made me wonder if

---

in his Nova Trilogy often references penny arcades with personal movie-viewing machines and movies of 1920. These two distinct elements are here blended together into a cinema-as-church, as perceived by an observer who had never seen movies before.

they were more like demons.[67]

But Gazma sure looked like heaven to me. It was the fine weather, the long summer lasting hundreds of days, the fields of growing grain, the orchards of beautiful fruit. And the Pleasure Domes for winter time, domes lined up like eggs in a carton.[68]

Still, Ayssa was there and I had to go, even if it was a one-way trip. Linn pledged to go, too. I tried to talk him out of it, at first, since he had his whole life ahead of him, then I just hoped he would change his mind at the last chance. Tilly[69] was not going to go all the way to Gazma — he would stop at Argyre, the last city.

Tilly was a blue man,[70] the first I had ever seen, and a pharmacist, a better one than myself. One day I happened

---

67. flickerman: ERB's Mars novel *Thuvia, Maid of Mars* (1920) has a type of psionic adept "etherialist" who can create phantom bowmen, send them out to fight enemies, and then dematerialize them when their mission is done. WSB's Nova Trilogy has a class of what might be called "film people," black and white images who stutter like movie sequences badly spliced or deteriorating through overuse, and at death they burn like nitrous filmstock.

68. Pleasure Domes: Alluding to the opening of "Kubla Khan" (1816) by Samuel Taylor Coleridge: "In Xanadu did Kubla Khan a stately pleasure dome decree." According to the poet, the poem was influenced by opium.

69. Tilly: Technical Tilly, a.k.a. Uranian Willy the Heavy Metal Kid, a character from WSB's *The Soft Machine*. While he is a member of the Nova Mob, he betrays them as "Willy the Rat."

70. blue man: WSB has blue men who are drug addicts from the planet Uranus. ERB has blue men of Jupiter, in "Skeleton Men of Jupiter" (1943), collected in *John Carter of Mars* (1964).

to talk to him about the possibilities of an alcohol substitute, a chemical compound that could deliver the pleasant effects without the katzenjammer. I was only chatting in an idle way, reflecting upon the alcohol restrictions in the cities along the Pilgrim Rise. That is, Ladon had nothing stronger than beer (the first beer I had even heard of on Jizma, by the way), and Uzboi had nothing more potent than small beer, and Argyre had no alcohol at all. So pilgrims were purifying themselves on the way up to Gazma.

Anyway, I was just chatting with Tilly about a synthetic alcohol improvement, but he became very serious and told me there was such a thing, called "Soma,"[71] and he was taking a load up to Argyre.

That is the thing — there is this strange contradiction. Even though the cities on the Pilgrim Rise were alcohol restricted, it turns out there was a thriving business of alcohol smuggling going on. It was like Freemasonry, or something. Practically an open secret. But for smuggling purposes, it made sense economically to carry high proof alcohol, the higher the better. The holier the cities became, the more they resembled the "Gin Lane" of the old engraving.[72]

Back then I still believed in the evils of alcohol. That is why I was trying to dream up a chemical solution. I was not an absolutist, though, and I tried a few of the beers. Not my cup of tea.

I was much more interested in the fizzy, non-alcoholic

---

71. Soma: Named after a religious drink of ancient India, Soma is best known as a widely used recreational drug in Huxley's novel *Brave New World* (1932).

72. William Hogarth's two prints "Beer Street" and "Gin Lane" (1751). The first depicts a utopia of health and good humor, the second portrays a dystopia of addiction and crime.

drinks — so many strange flavors that would never appear in the United States! There was one like pineapple, it tasted slightly fermented; another like salty-watermelon. There was one that seemed a coconut milk fizz, then a real milk fizz, as well as blackcurrant, mint, and banana. But all that is just trivia.

The fact is, I was in a deep funk after I found out I had lost the race, that Ayssa was already in Gazma. All of our hurrying around, checking places for her, burning up money in fast transportation, all was for nothing — she had already been on the underground river the whole time. "Orpheus unhappy by no fault of his."[73]

I fell into despair for a couple of days, maybe three. Everything just seemed so hopeless. Tilly offered me a dose of Soma, and I thought, "Why not?"

Would you not?[74]

So I took the stuff and after a while I felt this rising ebullience. It was not the stimulation of cocaine, or even coffee, for that matter. I have had experiences with ether that briefly show this effect with high doses. It is hard to explain, but it made the world of Jizma look better, and it made my situation look better — it gave me hope, and the spunk to shape my destiny. And just like Tilly said, there was no katzenjammer whatsoever.

Well, anyway, enough navel gazing. Back to the main story.

Life on the Pilgrim Rise becomes more and more expensive the higher one goes. The final stage is no exception, because every pilgrim has to have a watercraft

---

73. Lines 454-55 from Georgic IV, Vergil's poem on Orpheus.

74. This is an awkward, obscure call out to WSB's phrase "Wouldn't you?" from the Introduction to *Naked Lunch,* which immediately continues: "Yes you would. You would lie, cheat, inform on your friends, steal, do anything to satisfy total need."

of some kind to float down the last stretch of the canal, which goes underground. One might think a canoe would work, but it would not, since the trip lasts ten days or thereabouts. So there is the Pilgrim Raft, and it is expensive, but a group can get together to pool their money. Pilgrims who want to go in style and comfort take a Merchant Barge, and above that there is the Noble Scow.

Each pilgrim needs ten days' worth of food, rations that weigh around twelve pounds total, I guess. And ten days of drinking water. One needs a light source, and they sell a device that uses energy to create cold light for about six hours in total. It costs as much as a half man-day of rations, and one buys two at least. Then there are these little glow lights, like lightning bug stuff, that one has to put on points of the craft to act as warning lights. They only last a few days each, so one must buy multiples.

All told, this expense is the amount one would pay for ordinary food and lodging for an entire Earth month, but this is the bare minimum for a ten-day trip through inky blackness. And daily life is so expensive the further up the Return Canal one goes, it is hard to save enough for the send-off — especially if one did not budget for it from the beginning.

Our main source of income was Linn's fighting rooster,[75] who was the Glory of Koreh, but things became tough for him, too. He used to win combats without breaking a sweat, but now he was winded easily. Maybe it was the thinner air of the high elevation. In any event, he would flop over in the pit, and Linn would take him up, spit into his gaping beak. That was the first level of concern. Then came times when that technique was not enough, and Linn had to go the next step, where he would take the rooster's comb between his lips and suck blood into it. That was more serious. But then the last time, Linn

---

75. rooster: Link to *The Ticket That Exploded* (Ch. 12 and 15).

licked the eye clean and took the whole head into his mouth. It seemed to work — the Glory of Koreh popped out hard and spunky, full of vim and vigor, but he was dead a few strokes later.

So then we ran booze and Soma up the line, struggling along in a hard way. The further one takes it, the more it is worth, but we were just hired carriers.

To save money we quit going to temples. Well, also to avoid the flickermen. That did not stop the flickermen from dogging Tilly. There was the time Tilly shot the one, but the next time there were three. We managed to shoot our way out of that mess, but then I saw Tilly was wounded, bleeding out a silver blood that evaporated.

I said to him, "What is this?" But he said, "Shut up and listen." Then he told me the secret formula for Soma. He was coughing, gasping for breath. His last words were, "We shall meet again in Gazma."

I did not know what that meant. I asked Linn if Gazma was a place all spirits go to when Jizmatics die. He just shrugged, said it was confusing to him as well. Maybe it was common among blue men, that idea.

We sold the last of the Soma and the formula up at Argyre. Barely enough for a puny raft and all the supplies — we had to sell our guns, but it seemed we did not need those anymore, where we were going. Then we shoved off in a flotilla of pilgrims.

One cannot begin to imagine what it is like to be in the underground canal. At first I felt in my bones it would be light again in twelve hours, but then days go by in darkness. People around sing and joke, trying to keep their spirits up, but day after day of darkness beats everybody down. One loses all sense of time, except to minding the glow points of the raft.

Then the clock says one has reached the halfway point, and hope stirs within one, but then time slows down so that a minute stretches to an hour. And the water around the raft has become filthy with the wastes of all the pilgrims, so the canal has become a sanitary sewer.

"Who is the third who sits always beside you? When I count, there are only you and I together."[76]

"I do not know whether a man or woman — But who is that on the other side of you?"[77]

"Here," said she, "Is your card, the drowned Phoenician Sailor."[78]

I felt I was going mad. In order to cling to sanity and perhaps banish ghosts, I admitted my darkest secrets to Linn.

I said, "I am burdened by dark feelings. Ayssa, my beloved, your sovereign — on Pyosis [our planet Earth] she was also a queen. She had . . . husbands, two men, two great men. The first was Julius Caesar, the second was Marc Antony. She had children by both. On the one hand I am shamed that she has been married before and had children, but then I am awestruck since they were both such famous men. Then I am honored that she, who had known such as they, would choose me. Yet doubt creeps in, and I wonder if she thinks I am the transmitted form of Marc Antony — does she love me, or has she mistaken me for her true love?"

Linn thought about that for a while, then he asked if I had met either man.

I confessed I had not, since they had died long before my birth.

---

76. Adapted from T.S. Eliot's "The Waste Land" (lines 360–61).

77. Shaped from "The Waste Land" (lines 365–66).

78. Phoenician Sailor: Adapted from "The Waste Land," spoken by Madame Sosostris (lines 46–7). Curiously, a novel *The Wonderful Adventures of Phra the Phoenician* (1890) is considered by Richard A. Lupoff to have had a strong influence on ERB's *A Princess of Mars* (Lupoff, p. 24).

So Linn said, "Certes, her love for you must be plain, since upon losing you she took the pilgrimage from whence there is no return."

I appreciated what he said, but still, I had to tell him the rest of the story.

I said, "Aye, and there is the rub,[79] for that is what she did on Pyosis when she lost Marc Antony."

There was a time of uncomfortable silence. I regretted that I had halted our conversation, and I decided to start a new one.

I said, "I admit I am not clear on how the baby factories work."

Linn told me how a husband and wife apply for a baby. They pay their fees and each puts a hand into the slot, where a tiny bit of skin is taken. Their baby is started in a bottle. Two hundred and seventy days later, the baby is decanted.

I asked him if that was when they pick up their newborn.

He said, "No, the baby is cared for by nurses for two years."[80]

I did not know what to think. Four Earth years from conception to meeting? No, call it five Earth years. It seemed insane.

It was.[81]

---

79. Aye, and there is the rub: Modified from line in *Hamlet* (Act III, 1), a part of the famed "To be or not to be" soliloquy wherein Prince Hamlet considers suicide.

80. Martian birth and infancy: This is in line with ERB's system, described in chapter seven of *A Princess of Mars* (1912). It also looks a lot like the technology later used in Huxley's *Brave New World* (1932). Note that the "two years" are Martian years, each being about two Earth years.

81. This tunnel section seems like the opening lines of *The Ticket*

That Exploded: "It is a long trip. We are the only riders. So that is how we have come to know each other so well."

4 SLAVES OF AQUARIUS[82]

The glorious sunlight was too bright. With ten-day beards, Lee and Linn stumbled off the raft on legs weak from forced inactivity. On the shore, welcoming strangers handed them paper cups of fluid that they drank down with gratitude.

Instantly Lee felt a rush of bliss. Chemical Bliss. It was not the wonder of Soma: it was a far more powerful feeling of contentment, satisfaction.

Everything looked rosy and fine. The final pool with all the filth of the world was a marina during a festive regatta. The crab men breaking down the rafts and devouring pilgrims who had died along the way were like sporting porpoises. Lee was Linn and Linn was Lee, and they walked away from the water.

Up ahead were machines like cameras, boxy things on tripods. Leelinn[83] guessed that they were transmitting im-

---

82. Aquarius: The zodiac sign of the water carrier, which seems appropriate at the beating heart of the entire Martian canal system.

83. Leelinn: A nod to the sort of hybridization found in *The Soft*

ages of the recent arrivals to temples around the world. The other side of "Hello from Heaven."

The summer sun never sets in Gazma: it only circles around the horizon, which is why they call each twenty-four-hour period a "cycle." For Lee it was like an endless summer afternoon back at Harvard, and with the lack of night he came to realize it was just a single day that declined for all the hours of one hundred and fifty-three days.

The fields of Gazma were constantly being worked. Lee and Linn found themselves harvesting crops, eating slop that tasted fine, and sleeping in a tent of darkness.

Upon awakening they discovered that chemical Bliss delivered a hangover far worse than alcohol. They suffered cramps, fever, nausea, and crawling flesh. To escape this pain and misery, most workers poured their low wages into buying more Bliss. Just to stop the pain, just to restore a feeling of normalcy, one must take a minimum dose — call this the beer level. In order to feel the Bliss, one must take twice as much, the wine level, but this in turn raises the individual's minimum to the new level.[84]

In addition, it was a world of social pyramids, each stratum eating the one below, the lowest level being little more than walking skeletons.[85] The blues were at the top; the yellows were middle managers; the reds and the blacks were at the bottom.

Machine.

84. ERB did in fact write a novel involving opioid addiction: *The Girl from Hollywood* (1923), which vividly describes cravings, and mentions hypodermics three times.

85. From *Naked Lunch* appendix "Deposition: Testimony Concerning a Sickness," the line: "The pyramid of junk, one level eating the level below."

Lee showed talent and was promoted to Overseer, where his job was to push two dozen workers and sell them their Bliss. He would buy the stuff at the dispensary, staffed by yellows or blues who apparently never used it themselves.

Lee was promoted again, this time to Supplier. In a way Bliss in Gazma was similar to alcohol along the Pilgrim Rise, in that a schedule of dilution made the equivalent of beer, wine, fortified wine, et cetera. As his first Supplier job, Lee bought a quantity of twenty-four percent pure Bliss, then diluted it by one third to sixteen percent, the "fortified wine" level.[86] He sold this at good profit to overseers and advanced blissers, but he celebrated by drinking his own mix.

The "Bliss-sickness," the afterward illness, was terrible when it came. Alarmed, Lee tried a program of reduction, and sweated his way back down to the wine level.

One time at the dispensary, Lee was surprised to recognize a face from the Pilgrim Rise.

"Tilly!"

"Do I know you, Supplier?"

"It is I, Lee," said the Earthman. "William Lee."

"I am sorry, I know you not."

"You said we would meet again in Gazma. Or at least your double said that — he was some sort of flickerman."

"Oh," said the blue man. "I see. I think I understand. Let us find a place to sit down, and you can tell me everything."

When Lee told of the Soma selling, Tilly's face showed shock.

"No, not Soma!"

"Yes," said Lee, puzzled, "and he gave me the formula."

---

86. Dilution schedules gleaned from Barry Miles, *Call Me Burroughs: A Life*, p. 142.

"But you kept the formula secret, did you not?"

"No, you — Tilly — he told me to sell it. His dying breath. So I sold it. Why do you react this way?"

"Because it is doom."

"I do not see how," said Lee. "It doesn't give a katzenjammer like alcohol or this Bliss stuff."

"That is why it is doom. A weapon of last resort."

•

Tilly, this second Tilly, taught Lee many things. For example, while Lee knew that the green men are from Puuntango, our planet Venus, Tilly told him the blue men are from Rekmyook,[87] our planet Uranus. He went on to say, "They have worked out a co-dominium on Jizma, with the blues handling the Bliss and the greens handling the birth."

"You mean they handle the local baby factory?"

"No," said Tilly, "they control all the baby factories on Jizma."

"How is that possible, when nobody can leave Gazma?"

"They use flickermen to perform the mysteries at every baby factory."

"I cannot see how this works," said Lee.

"The blues run the farming in Gazma," said Tilly, "which is necessary for lasting through the winter. The blues also run the temples across Jizma, making flickers and inviting pilgrims."

"What do the blues get out of it?"

"Access to the Pleasure Domes during the winter."

"So both groups have worldwide enterprises — the blues have every temple, and the greens have every birth

---

87. Rekmyook: Apparently a coined word with no obvious relevance to the naming convention of "Jizma."

factory. And the blues also have the Pilgrim Way. So in reality there are two gods for Jizma, the god of Bliss and the god of birth."

"Yes, that is it," said Tilly. "It is all about control, the kind of control that relies upon slavery in one form or another. That is why it is important that you give me any message or formula from flickerman Tilly."

"I told you all I know."

"His mission was to find a cure for Bliss."

"We never spoke of it," said Lee. "I had no idea of it — nobody on Jizma knows, outside of Gazma. If they knew, the whole thing would collapse."

"Think back. You spoke with him about pharmaceutical chemistry. He must have said something."

"I cannot think," said Lee. "I am feeling sick. Give me some Bliss and I shall try."

"If I give you Bliss, you will not be able to focus."

"I can, I am sure I can. It is the pain right now that keeps me from focusing."

•

On the day the sun touched the horizon in the north at midnight, Tilly outlined a plan to Lee.

"I have tried experiments," said Tilly. "Myself and a few others. Nothing seems to work. Lately we have put everything into finding something that will be, in effect, an antidote to the poison.

"Let us try a reduction regimen upon you. From past trials, it seems that sixty cycles is too long. It is not the intensity but the duration of pain that breaks the will to resist. I propose a period of ten cycles, during which we will reduce by ten percent each dose."

"It cannot be that easy," said Lee.

They tried it.

Lee sweated, and Tilly showed tremendous patience, but the experiment failed when they could not break through the "beer" level to the "small beer" level. The beer level was a solid floor.[88]

•

"Here is some news," said Tilly. "Ayssa of Koreh has been elevated to the greens."

"Where is she?"

"Somewhere in the Pleasure Domes."

"I have to go see her."

"That is impossible at this time, but it is easy when winter is near."

"I will find a way in, I will break in!"

"You will not be able to find your way through the maze. Listen to me — you will not go in alone, but with an army at your back."

"What do you mean?"

"Exactly what I said. But we need to recruit that army, and to do that we need the antidote to Bliss."

•

After a break of ten cycles, during which the sun would disappear behind the northern edge every cycle for a white night twilight period, Tilly proposed a new regimen.

"A prolonged sleep," he said, "allowing the body to expel the toxins."

"Go to sleep sick, and wake up cured?"

"Yes. Five cycles of sleep and ten cycles of rest."

They put Lee into deep sleep for five cycles, but when they brought him back to consciousness they had a nasty surprise. The symptoms of Bliss-sickness had not been reduced, they had been multiplied. Added to this was the

---

88. A character in *The Girl from Hollywood* tries a reduction cure on her own (Ch. 15) and fails.

hangover from the sedative. The result was a syndrome of unparalleled horror.[89]

"The failed cure is worse than the disease!" cried Lee.

Another interval passed. The daylight was getting shorter and shorter as the solar disc circled lower and lower in the north. Tilly had worked up a formula of anti-Bliss.

"I propose we try this regimen," he said. "In seven cycles you will be free from Bliss. We will give you minute amounts of anti-Bliss every two hours, around the cycle."

At only five hours in, Lee said, "This cure is worse than the disease."

"No, my friend. It is just the usual sickness, is it not?"

Grudgingly, Lee admitted that to be true.

"But why have any symptoms at all?"

"They are reduced to an endurable level, are they not?"

"I suppose."

"That seems the best we can achieve."

It was a horrible sleepless nightmare. For the first cycle Tilly and his nurses seemed brutal and repugnant. Lee felt they were torturing him with sadistic glee and would eventually kill him. Everything looked blue. Inanimate objects seemed to stir with a writhing furtive life, alive and threatening.[90]

After five cycles, Lee at last fell asleep. Even so, he was

---

89. From *Naked Lunch* appendix "Letter from a Master Addict to Dangerous Drugs," "Prolonged Sleep" section, the line: "The end result was a combined syndrome of unparalleled horror."

90. From *Naked Lunch* appendix "Letter from a Master Addict to Dangerous Drugs," the line: "Familiar objects seem to stir with a writhing furtive life." Later, "for 24 hours the nurses and the doctor 'seemed brutal and repugnant.' And everything looked blue."

awakened every four hours for his next dose of anti-Bliss.[91]
And then, at the end of the seventh cycle, Lee said:
"Tilly, my good man, we have broken the lotus!"[92]

---

91. This technique based upon the apomorphine cure alluded to in the *Naked Lunch* appendix "Deposition . . ." and spelled out in Miles, p. 285. Thus, this section incorporates appendix material into the main body.

92. The "lotus eaters" being a strange people in Homer's *The Odyssey* (book IX).

5 OF DIS THE INFERNAL PALACE[93]

So when the sun sets on Gazma, summer is over, and everyone is evacuated into the Pleasure Domes. Now, the flickers give the idea that people frolic and play the whole winter long, but that is not true for most, only for the Beautiful People. The rest, and I was one of them, each get a narrow bunk and an injection of something that suspends the passage of time for hundreds of days. Solves the problem of seasonal labor, I guess. It looks like a dim catacomb full of the peaceful dead, but the experience is that time speeds up and gravity becomes nearly crushing so one cannot rise up. I only felt that way for a little while before Tilly gave me the antidote.

Things would have been simple if Ayssa had been warehoused like most of us were, but alas, she was a Beautiful People. She was living the advertised life of the Pleasure Domes, while we were skulking in the shadows, using forged papers identifying us as staff members.

Our first task was to recruit an army. I did not mention this before, but Tilly had told me he was an agent from a

---

93. Line 467 of Vergil's Georgic IV.

galactic police force, and that the Jizmatic operations using birth and Bliss were criminal enterprises from Venus and Uranus.

So then, recruiting an army from a catacomb of the comatose goes this way. First we would identify a potential recruit among the sleepers, based upon the word of agents who knew that person. We would give him the antidote, and if he would not join we would send him back to sleep.

We established secret places wherein to give the anti-Bliss cure to our new agents. This operation took seven cycles, about an Earth week, and required a lot of man-power support.

But in the meantime we had found our way into the complex from whence are sent all the wireless trans-missions to temples across Jizma. I myself piloted a flickerman, which is something like working a marionette, but there are more forms of flickermen than I had sup-posed at first.

Anyway, I walked in Argyre as a phantom, and found it had become a ghost town. Tilly was right — the Soma had destroyed the place. Among other things, this meant the water was not flowing uphill anymore. "And, the wind hushed, Ixion's wheel stood still."[94]

My main goal was to contact Doctor Benway. We needed his help. I remembered his project for making an army of synthetic men, and now that we had access to the birth factories, it seemed possible we could help him in that. But the first thing was to find him, and he was in hiding.

•

---

94. Line 484 from Georgic IV. Because the mortal Ixion [ik-SIGH-on] attempted adultery with the goddess Hera, he was sentenced to punishment on an ever-turning wheel in the underworld. It halted briefly as Orpheus worked his skill.

When I finally caught up with Ayssa it was in a quiet corner, you can be sure. She recognized me right away, gave a gasp of "Isis!" and the tears started to flow.

I gave her a hug, told her a brief outline of the situation.

She asked me how we would get out of this infernal place.

I said it would be Jizma or Earth, but we were getting out.

She said, "Earth? But how?"

I told her my fallback plan, that if all else failed and we could not get out of Gazma, I would shoot her dead, then kill myself.

She was shocked, repulsed by the idea.

I explained it to her. I said, "When I died here on Jizma, I returned to my body on Earth. I think the same would happen for you. Darling, I found your body, and right now my body is lying next to it. We can die here and wake up together in Alexandria."

She said, "You mean . . . all this time . . . I could have returned?"

I told her she had no way of knowing, and besides it might not work. But it had worked for me before. It was our ace in the hole.

•

Tilly told me, "Always keep in mind that you are operating under conditions of guerrilla war. For example, never try to hold a position under massive counterattack."

I was at a cafe. I could feel the heat moving in,[95] pressure rising like a sign of summer storm. A crabman came into the place, a monstrous six-foot-tall horseshoe crab

---

95. Beginning of opening line for *Naked Lunch:* "I can feel the heat closing in . . ."

walking upright on two legs like a man. Armored within his whitish-grey shell, he was clomping along, peering around with his beady little pig eyes, but the claws — one always saw the claws, big vicious things, even when one was not looking at them. He had four smaller arms on his chest — these were good for taking documents and bribes.

It was time, so I drew my pistol and blasted him, but his carapace seemed immune to disruptor beam. He lowered his stance and charged at me for a headbutt that I dodged at the last second. As he looked up, his mouth a vertical slit of needle teeth, I shot him in the face and this time his protein dissolved.

Then I ran out onto the street, right into the arms of a flying scorpion man who must have been the other's partner. His stinger thrust at me, but I parried it with my pistol and a spurt of poison splashed against my skin without effect. Two shots and he was dead.

There was a green boy sitting at the gutter and I could tell he was being ridden by another who was located somewhere else. I pointed my gun at him and said, "Show me your controller quick or I kill you."

He nodded and opened up a scroll that had moving images. I saw a woman's face, but not just any woman.

It was Koyotel, the Aztec girl who had become Queen of Freedonia. She saw me, too, and snarled, "Die, Conquistador! Die!"

I had her location now, and I called it out over the wireless. The flickerman army knew which spider hole she was hiding in. I kept the scroll so I could watch her be captured or killed.[96]

•

---

96. This episode is modeled on *The Ticket That Exploded* (Ch. 11) section "combat troops in the area."

The dome was broken in this place, shattered by heavy ordnance between the ceasefires, and snow was drifting down.

EPILOGUE

This is flickerman William Lee, giving an update on Agent Lee. After the successful storming of the Reality Laboratory,[97] Lee and his men cornered the Arch Scientist. Agent Lee offered free passage in exchange for the woman Ayssa, but the criminal shouted defiance and retreated with Ayssa into what appeared to be a closet. According to Tilly it is a sort of elevator that goes down for miles.

Lee and others took the remaining car down. The rest of us remain here, trying to stabilize Gazma and restore the flow along the Return Canal.

Flickerman William Lee, over and out.[98]

---

97. Reality Laboratory: A reference to "reality studio" in WSB's *Nova Express* (1964), a media-industrial complex that creates an ersatz reality in order to manipulate and control people.

98. Overthrowing false religions: "The Mayan Caper," chapter 7 of WSB's *The Soft Machine* (1961), is a miniature of that novel's main plot, with one secret agent setting out to destroy a murderously evil false religion. This in turn exhibits a strong parallel to ERB's *The Gods of Mars* (serialized 1913).

Secret Master of Jizma[99]

---

99. This title approximates *The Warlord of Mars* (serialized 1913–14), ERB's conclusion of the Martian trilogy.

INTRODUCTION (1914) BY NORMAN LEE BEAN

Once upon an evening stormy in the month of late September I found my mood becoming dreary as I stared at dying embers. My daily woes I set aside, and thought instead on one away who either lived or else had died: my Uncle Bill, for whom I pray.[100]

The world he left behind again has changed in ways I scarce can count. His formulas now lost to Man, the sorry fate of all his work.

But then I thought about his college chum Teddy, who, during his period of national service, proved instrumental in starting the American Panama Canal Project in 1903. Some time after Teddy left office, a would-be assassin shot him, yet the next year Teddy set out as co-leader for an expedition into the heart of the Amazon, searching for the

---

100. This paragraph closely echoes the language of Poe's "The Raven" without actually quoting it.

source of the River of Doubt.[101]

Just last April this expedition emerged from the jungle, and a near-death Teddy received medical treatment at Manaós. A month later saw his return to the United States, where he enjoyed a hero's welcome in New York Harbor. Such a happy day that was.

But then in June an assassination set Europe ablaze, and by July this fire had grown to a General War. Last month the Panama Canal opened in the New World, but in the Old World a German zeppelin bombed a French city from the air.

A knocking at my front door interrupted my musings upon such somber matters. Answering that summons, I found three men on my doorstep: one of them looked so familiar that I cried out in surprise, "Uncle Bill!"

"Yes and no," said that man. "May we come in?"

As you have no doubt already guessed, dear reader, this was not my uncle Doctor William Lee, but an agent of his who was a photographic double. The trio of far travelers wanted something from me, and I asked questions of them. We conversed in such manner all night in my living room, resulting in this, the latest dispatch from distant Jizma.[102]

— Norm L. Bean

---

101. Apparently "Teddy" is Theodore Roosevelt, U.S. President (1901–09) and a leader of the Roosevelt-Rondon Scientific Expedition (1913–14) exploring the thousand-mile long River of Doubt, subsequently renamed Roosevelt River.

102. Visitors from another world: In the frame tale to ERB's novel *The Gods of Mars* the hero from the red planet visits ERB himself in 1898 to give him written notes that would become the novel in 1913.

1 BATTLE TO THE INNER SANCTUM

Following the sounds of combat, William Lee led his team through six chambers hazy with lingering gun smoke and stained with splatters of blood. At last they came upon a site of fierce struggle. The hated guards were massed at the entrance to a great chamber where they were attempting to halt the further progress of liberators toward the inner sanctum of the laboratory.

Lee lobbed a grenade at the guards with the cry, "For Koreh!" The liberators took heart at the sound of his voice and the arrival of reinforcements. Before the guards could recover from their temporary demoralization their ranks were broken and the liberators had burst into the chamber.

The fight within that room was a testament to the grim ferocity of Jizma's warlike people. The liberators battled there that day against the old guard. No man asked quarter or gave it. They fought for their very lives.

All knew that the fate of Jizma would hinge forever upon the outcome of this battle. It was a clash between the new and the old, but Lee did not question the outcome of it. He fought side by side with the liberators for their total emancipation from the throttling bondage of a seductive superstition, a Faustian bargain.

Then the liberators punched through into the inner sanctum, with Lee in front and Linn right behind him. From further inside the bowels of the laboratory came a female cry, unmistakably that of Lee's beloved Ayssa, and she was near. Lee dodged to the corridor wall where he crouched and shouted, "Your lives for the Queen — that is my offer!"

In response came only laughter, mirthless and cruel, followed by the sound of scuffling. Were the blue men trying to execute their hostage?

Lee led the charge into the final room, a chamber with two elevator doors. One was open and he saw three arch-scientists pulling Ayssa into the car with them, while remaining guards let loose a blistering fire. Ayssa screamed, the door closed, and the fight began for the other car, with the guards trying to get there first.

The skirmish was quickly won. Lee rushed into the remaining car, finding it to be a round room with bolted-down chairs facing the door and a wall with a closet at the back. Linn ran in, as did the other companions, but Lee gestured to a flickerman to stay behind, commanding him, "Gather reinforcements and follow as soon as you can!"

Lee jabbed the button. The flickerman saluted. The doors closed and the car began moving downward.

The men waited, primed for sudden combat, but the sinking kept on at a steady pace. Looking around the compartment, Lee found above the doors a chronometer counting down from twelve hours. This seemed to imply a dozen hours for the trip. Exploring the car, they found a cupboard with hardtack foodbars as well as a compact water closet, which made the vehicle more like a stateroom on an ocean liner.

The chairs were unusual in having belts built into them. These mysterious belts could be used to fasten a sitter into place. The chairs could also be reclined into couches.

The men each lay down upon a couch and tried to rest for the coming battle. Lee slept fitfully, awakening each time to see the timepiece had not moved as much as he hoped.

In the last thirty minutes Lee jumped up with nervous energy, unable to take the wait any longer. He paced around like a caged animal, checking and re-checking his weapons. A bell rang the moment the chronometer hit the final ten-minute mark.

Lee stretched his limbs and paced by the door. Linn urged him to take his couch, pointing to a couch symbol that had appeared in a little window by the timepiece, but Lee refused, wanting to be able to leap out the door the instant it opened.

The final minute found the bell ringing continuously. Lee crouched by the door . . .

And the floor fell away from his feet!

Tumbling forward, his body slammed into the door, a sharp pain to his right arm.

His pistol left his hand to fall up and then down.

Lee, crumpled on the floor by the door, felt the elevator going up, but it had never stopped moving. Linn helped him to stand, discovering that Lee's arm was broken.

The chronometer was now counting up.

The men had no splints for Lee's arm, but he took a pain killer. They talked over theories of what had happened. It seemed unlikely that they had passed through the center of the planet in twelve hours, since that implied a speed greater than one hundred and seventy-five miles per hour, far in excess of what they thought their speed was. But if they had passed through the world then presumably they would emerge at the north, in the Arctic Circle, where it would be summer.

In some ways it seemed as though the car had made a U-turn, like a ball bearing going through the arm of a trombone, in which case they would arrive somewhere back in Jizma's Antarctic Circle.

Once again they had twelve hours to agonize over it.

When the chronometer reached 11:50, a bell rang, just as before, but this time the couch symbol was not revealed.

At 11:58 the car began to slow. The men tensed in two pairs beside the door, flanking it for those remaining minutes.

The car came to a gentle stop. The doors opened to a dim red light and a bizarre landscape they could not have guessed: suspended in the sky above like a big red sun was a thing like a skinned pomegranate in which the jeweled seeds of one hemisphere cast light of varying intensity while the other hemisphere was dark. This infernal, leprous sun cast a spotty daylight upon skylands beyond, city-dotted continents with dark seas between them.

Just as Lee realized the impossible truth, that they were inside of a hollow Jizma,[103] he and his men were gunned down.

The last thing he heard was Ayssa screaming his name and weeping.

---

103. hollow Jizma: The ERB novel *At the Earth's Core* (1914), first of the Pellucidar series, is set in a "hollow Earth." ERB later depicted a "hollow Moon" with *The Moon Maid* (1926). Having established this pattern, it seems a logical step to a "hollow Mars." However, ERB's Pellucidar is a world that has no night, experiencing instead a permanent "timeless" noon; adding the trope of a leprous sun is a turn of difference.

2 A STRANGE ANCIENT WORLD

"Remember, Cleo. We had our pact." Sprawled on a dirty divan, smirking at him with again the last vapor of the ethereal vision. It was plain. "No, my husband will come soon!" He had turned increasingly to adventure. "My friend is guarding the door." Her current girth repulsed him, and he "Wait, wait! Tell me more." His bride until a few weeks back he chanced upon we are here. We have bodies. There a Gibson Girl[104] he used to know. What was Hades? The hag knew it.[105]

---

104. Gibson Girl: Iconic illustrations of American female beauty for twenty years beginning in the 1890s, she is at ease and stylish, yet athletic. Drawn by Charles Dana Gibson, connected to the romances of Robert Chambers, the forgotten fluff that made him a commercial success.

105. This paragraph is an example of "cut up," the well-known WSB technique of combining material from two separate pages. While it might seem too modern for a work of 1914, Robert Chambers hit something similar with his "The Prophets' Paradise" section of prose poetry in *The King in Yellow* (1895).

•

"Wake up."

The words came to William Lee out of a nightmare filled with discordant sounds. He tried to sit up, but the pain made him lie back down again with a groan. He coughed, and pain coursed through his chest, along his broken arm. He opened gummy eyes and saw a black scientist towering over him where he lay on the floor of a small room.

"Good," said the man. "Now get up." The man knelt down and tugged upward on Lee's good arm.

"Where to?" gasped Lee as he struggled to rise.

"To meet the lord."

Lee shuffled after the man whose white tunic looked so much like a lab coat. When they exited the shack, Lee saw the leprous sun hanging in the center of the sky, but the bulb overhead was still dark. Looking back at the shack in the twilight darkness, he saw it stood hidden within an outcropping of boulders.

Lee followed the scientist across a sandy stretch toward a cliff face. This bluff had a series of holes that Lee took to be nesting spots for birds until he surmised they were windows for human inhabitants.

Lee assumed it was the mansion of the lord, but when they walked into the wide entryway he sensed the place was more a stable than a house. Yet instead of quadrupeds there was a trio of gasbags, the biggest being six feet across. Puzzled, Lee followed his guide across the room, and the hair on his neck stood up when he heard the bags gibbering to each other.

At the far end of the room the man led him down stairs cut into the stone and lit by radium bulbs. Lee tried asking questions of his guide but was always rebuffed. After descending for some time they emerged in a large cavern filled by a lake, and they followed the right-hand path around it.

They passed a tunnel mouth on the right. On the

opposite side of the lake was a cleft, their destination. When they arrived, Lee appraised the lord's domicile as worthy of a hermit researching natural philosophy in a place far removed from the distractions of civilization. A man sat at a desk, looking over a scroll among many. A pale man, he, too, wore a white tunic, but he would never be mistaken for Roger Bacon[106] as his head was mis-shapen, nearly like that of a circus freak, and his thick beard was blue in color.

"My lord," said the guide by way of introduction, "here be yer guest."

The leader looked over in surprise, and then smiled broadly, exposing his twisted, repulsive teeth.

"Ah, ye live," he said.

"Yes, thanks to you."

"We shall get to that, by and by. Ye were the only one to survive, left for dead amongst yer friends three. We thought ye dead, as well, but in looting the bodies, Ghin-spok here discovered some hint of life to ye, so along we brought ye."

"The blue men, the ones who ambushed us, where are they?"

"They be on the long road to Gnydon. Do ye know it?"

Lee shook his head. "I must follow them."

"Ye be in no condition to do such thing. Look at ye! Besides, they be several days away."

"Several days!" cried Lee. He made a rapid calculation, and then asked, "Has no one else come from the elevators?"

"No. Do ye expect others a-coming from the outer side?"

"I assume so. I hope so."

---

106. Roger Bacon: A medieval philosopher. Like Vergil, he was later considered a wizard.

"And be ye strangers to the Intersphere?"

"Yes, we are."

"Ah. Things be different here, very clear and direct. Few things in life here be free. It be tough, but fair. O my guest, what be yer name?"

"William Lee."

"I be sage Kamurder. This be my associate, the alchemist Ghinspok. Ye owe me for saving yer life, worth about four hours of sunlight. To pay off this debt, I propose that ye ingest a few of our test medications."

Lee considered carefully before saying, "But if I do this I will be even further behind in my pursuit."

"I will arrange for ye to be transported ahead of them. They go afoot, but ye will fly."

·

Lee quickly learned about the sacrifice economy of the Intersphere.[107] The most basic form was sunlight: a human sacrifice would provide the area of a city-state with four hours of sunlight from the overhead node of the leprous sun. Most cities would commit four per day: one for morning at six o'clock, two for midday at ten o'clock, and the final for afternoon at two o'clock.

In addition to the impersonal solar nodes there was a vast array of gods, some in charge of natural elements such as rivers and storms, while others rewarded various and sundry vices. Kamurder declared that all these gods were evil, some more than others, yet they were required for civilization, even life itself. The ones who stood in opposition to them were the Sacrilegious, from rough nomads of the wastelands to technologists cloistered in

---

107. Intersphere: Alluding to WSB's "Interzone," the dystopian international zone of Tangier, Morocco, mentioned in *Naked Lunch*.

obscure monasteries.

To avoid any association with the latter, Kamurder professed himself a staunch neutral. Because his main industry was founded upon a subterranean fungus forest, he did not subscribe to the hungry sun, leaving his area in perpetual twilight. The fungus provided the raw material for his medical chemicals. He also had a Bliss farm, tended by a few dozen yellow-skinned addicts. For Lee this last detail was a little too close to the situation he had fought against in Gazma, but it paled when compared to the sacrifice economy.

The agreement was that Lee would ingest three different compounds on three separate days and report on their effects. After completing this task he would be fitted to one of the living gasbags that would, upon being released, unerringly fly to its spawning grounds near the city-state of Gnydon.

At the first trial, Lee felt nothing but a mild pain reduction to his wounded body. During the second trial he found his heart racing uncontrollably, in the grip of a powerful stimulant. The third experience was a vague euphoria with minor hallucinations of an amusing nature.

Believing his assignment was completed, Lee asked for his ride to the city and god of Gnydon. Kamurder refused, saying they had not yet succeeded. Lee, angry at this shift in the deal, asserted his own pharmaceutical skill and asked them what they were trying to make.

Their goal was a synthetic version of a rare root. They remained silent as to its effects, but they suggested this root was somehow necessary to the entire operation. Sage Kamurder desired the ability to manufacture an adequate substitute at will.

Lee requested a dose of the root so that he might analyze it. They gave him a dust-like powder of such tiny amount it might fit inside a sesame seed. With a pin he divided it in half, then one half into half again. These few specks he put onto his tongue, employing the method used on Earth from ancient times to Newton.

Borrowing a quill and papyrus, he jotted notes on the chemical elements he detected. He noticed a flush of health, as if his wounds and bones were healing. He felt energetic, even a little restless, and continued his note writing.

Someone entered the chamber. Lee looked up and beheld a radiantly beautiful woman, a glowing goddess. The other men seemed unaware, so Lee wondered if this was a hallucination. Her skin looked as smooth as silk, and her curves were so alluring that he felt compelled to stand up and reach toward her.

The men, startled by this, moved to restrain Lee. The bluebeard shouted at the woman, who simpered, turned coquettishly, and left the area.

Lee was enraged. He wanted to go with that woman. He struggled pathetically against the two men, wishing he could kill them and follow after Ayssa.

Someone stuck him with a pin and he felt a change. With the antidote the sudden health and energy proved false by leaving so quickly he nearly fell over. Though his flesh was weak, his spirit remained strong, and he pushed away the hands to follow Ayssa.

The next room was a dead end.

"Where did she go?" he croaked to Kamurder and Ghinspok.

"What mean ye?" asked the alchemist. "Right there she be."

He was pointing at the slave crone who made some feeble gestures at cleaning the room.

Lee stared at the hag. This raddled addict, all skin and bones, had appeared to him as bewitching as a goddess, as alluring as Ayssa. He felt his gorge rise: the slave was practically a corpse.

3 REVOLTING TRIALS

Working like a man possessed, Lee crafted a drug, then announced this to the others before collapsing from exhaustion.

Some time later Ghinspok woke him and told him to help set up the trial. Earthman followed alchemist out to the underground lake, then onto the dock. At the dock's end Ghinspok commented on the low level of the water, but Lee was preoccupied by the eldritch items revealed by rays from the alchemist's radium lamp: a Saint Andrew's Cross facing the lake, and a crystal coffin.[108] When Ghinspok put down the lamp beside the latter, its light showed a body inside, blurred by a semi-transparent substance.

Ghinspok produced a key that unlocked the coffin. The corpse contained within was that of a woman, white of skin, golden of hair. The black man told him to get her out and bring her around to the front of the wooden X. Lee reminded him of his broken arm. Ghinspok reached into the cloudy slime and pulled the body out, the slime retreating in an animal way. He carried the cadaver around to the

---

108. crystal coffin: A trope of fairy tales such as "Snow White."

cross, leaned it upright against the wood, and told Lee to hold it in place.

Lee did so, and studied the body as Ghinspok ran a chain across its chest from armpit to armpit. She had died young, scarcely older than a child. Her hair was long. The corpse was supple, as if recently deceased. The neck showed a reddish band of almost bruising. Ghinspok fixed the wrists to manacles on the upper arms of the cross, and then fixed the ankles to manacles on the lower arms. The body hung there, trussed, with chin down.

Kamurder joined them, wearing only a sybaritic robe. He glanced at the corpse, and then strode to a corner of the dock that had a metal pole as if for the mooring of a boat. The sage took up a small mallet chained there and struck the pole with a measured pattern: three, one, four, one, five.

There was a stirring of something deep in the lake, then the alchemist and the sage turned to study the corpse expectantly.

Lee felt the silence grow eerie. Then the hair rose on his neck as a sob — low, gentle, but very distinct — came from the corpse. Lee strained his vision to detect any motion from the body, but there was nothing. Kamurder took his dose of the new drug. Lee looked back to the cadaver and saw a slight, feeble, and barely noticeable tinge of color had flushed up within the cheeks, and along the sunken small veins of the eyelids.

Then came a tremor upon the lips. Lee shuddered, seeing a partial glow upon the forehead and upon the cheek and mottled throat, a slight pulsation at the breast.[109]

The drug's effects were taking hold of Kamurder. He shrugged off the robe and advanced upon the re-animated girl. For her part, she opened eyes filled with the dull

---

109. These details seem inspired by Edgar Allan Poe's story "Ligeia" (1838).

horror of facing a recurrent nightmare, but when she saw Lee, a desperate hope flickered across her young face. Lee flinched as he received a telepathic message from her:

Stranger from another world, have mercy! Please kill me in a manner more permanent. Cut off my head, or remove my heart. I beg ye!

Kamurder practiced unspeakable vileness upon the chained prisoner. The worm of the lake, a neutral god, witnessed the abominable rites. At the end of the defilement, Kamurder looped the golden hair thrice around her neck and strangled the life out of her.

With the girl's death came a gurgling sound from the lake. Lee saw an upflow of currents near the middle.

"Well done," said Kamurder, clapping him on the shoulder. "Better than the old root. In the morning ye shall fly."

Lee was stupefied. As Kamurder staggered away, Lee helped Ghinspok take down the cadaver and put it back into the coffin.

Afterwards Lee was unable to sleep, tossing and turn-ing on his sleeping furs and silks. The depravity of a "neutral" god sickened him. He was glad to have won his flight, but haunted by the girl's request. The more he thought on her plight, the worse he felt. Finally he was moved to action.

He rose and padded silently through the sleeping household, then out to the dock. The coffin's lock was fairly simple and he picked it in about five minutes. After lifting the lid, he paused, testing the edge of his knife against his thumb. Then he was inspired by a new thought.

Using mainly his good arm, he manhandled the corpse again upon the X. The water level was higher now, and the lake was full. Lee used the mallet to tap the pattern on the pipe. Grimly he waited, preparing himself to mutilate the body if he must, but again came the hackle-raising death sob. The girl was breathing. Her eyes opened and Lee saw in them confusion, then happiness, followed by anxiety.

"Kill me, please," she said.

"No," he said. "Escape with me."

The robe was still there, so he put it on her. Her legs gave out, so he carried her on his back, off the dock, around the lake, and up the stairs. At the stables he set her down and asked how to ride the gasbags. She told him each could carry a man. She showed him how to fit the saddle onto one so that it hung below the sphere like a child's swing.

Lee wasted precious time trying to tie the saddles together into a basket for two. Then he released the smallest of the three gasbags outside, where it puffed up and flew away.

"Why?" she asked.

"To keep Kamurder from following," he said.

She laughed drily. "That man will be the least of yer worries. Ye have angered a god."

"I feel bad," said Lee. "He saved my life."

Lee used a twenty-foot length of rope, one end tied around his waist, the other around hers. Then they led the gasbags out, holding their saddle cords and ready to sit in their seats.

Once outside, the gasbags gave a joyous sound and began expanding rapidly. First they were double sized, then they were triple sized, and then Lee found they were airborne. He was surprised that he had not felt even the acceleration of an elevator, yet in seconds they were hundreds of feet up.

The gasbags rose up through different layers of air currents until they found a wind blowing in the favored direction, whereupon they rode that river of air. The balloonists travelled south on a night wind express, the distant skylands in daylight with the ragged edge of dawn approaching their longitude.

They flew over farms where dogs barked at their passage. They were over a city-state with a forbidding pyramid where a priest cut out a man's heart, and the solar node overhead came on like a light bulb. In the quasi-morning light Lee saw a line below and knew it must be the road along which Ayssa and her captors had traveled.

Lee studied the terrain rolling along. By picking a feature and seeing how long it took to fly past it, he estimated that they were moving at around ten miles an hour.

Lee and the girl maintained silence in the understanding that their voices could be heard below as easily as they could hear everything from the ground. And so they floated along as quiet as a cloud, sixteen feet apart, their gasbags bumping.

They passed over another city-state, then over farms that gave way to a swamp. Lee's rapt attention to the ground was suddenly interrupted by a strange cough from the girl, and then the rope around his waist nearly jerked him off his seat. The other gasbag was moving up and away, while the girl dangled below him on the tether, the increased weight forcing his balloon to sink rapidly.

Lee called to the girl. She did not respond, and seemed unconscious. He strained at lifting the rope foot by foot, his broken arm screaming with pain. At last, sweat in his eyes, he held her and found she was dead. She seemed to be decaying before his eyes.

The gasbag's continuing descent brought him out of his stunned paralysis. Lee realized he had to drop her body to stay afloat, and his fingers worked at the knot around the corpse.

Treetops, once so far away, were rushing up at him. He was making progress, the knot was beginning to budge, only a few more seconds, but then things flew by and there was a thump above his head. He saw an arrow in the side of the gasbag. The gasbag gave a mournful cry and two more arrows pierced it, then everything fell and Lee was knocked out.

4 THE END OF IT ALL

Ghinspok was surprised by a team of technological soldiers, and shocked as he recognized their leader.

"Ye must have a lot of brass," he said, "coming back here after what ye done."

"Tell me more," said the other.

•

William woke with a twitch.

He lifted his face from the wooden table where his body slumped. Wiping his mouth, he took in the immediate surroundings of a rundown room in a tropical clime. But there was something else, a vision fading like a snowflake on a hot skillet, a disappearance that gave him a mysterious sense of loss, feeling like a missing tooth. The mighty Amazon, father of . . .

"Well, look who is back," croaked a voice off to the side.

He turned to see the hag, his wife, sprawled on a dirty divan, smirking at him with contempt. Cruel reality shouldered aside the last vapor of the ethereal vision. It was plain as pain that across the decades of their marriage he had turned increasingly to adventure while she had turned progressively to alcohol. Her current girth repulsed him, and he could not remember the girlish form of his bride[110] until a few weeks back he chanced upon an expatriate woman half his age. Deja[111] vu of a Gibson Girl he used to know. What was her name? He had chased this nymph on a side trip,[112] and the hag knew it. His "adventuring" had become so dirty and dishonest, lecherous rather than heroic. In revenge the hag had begun an affair with Ka-murder. William had all of the grief and none of the joy, since the young woman had proved as phantasmal as the recently departed dream vision.

The time had come for change.

William stood up, and wobbling, awkwardly braced himself against the table.

"Whoa, pard," cackled the hag. "Where you going, Bill?"

"Time for us to go home," he said. "To the States."

"Need money for that, Bill."

"Going to sell my pistol."

Out the door, along the threadbare hallway, down the

---

110. Marriage trouble: ERB's 34-year-marriage to Emma was crumbling in 1934. ERB's chief complaints seem to have been her becoming overweight and alcoholic (Porges, p. 556). The divorce would come on December 6th.

111. Deja: First half of name for "Dejah Thoris," the princess of Mars. "Déjà vu" (French for "already seen") has the haunting quality that hints at precognition of future events and/or dimly recalled past events via reincarnation.

112. side trip: This relates to WSB, whose 5-year-marriage to Joan was crumbling in 1951. He had taken a side trip to hunt yage for several weeks, and had reason to suspect she had been unfaithful during his absence.

flyspecked stairwell, his shoulder rubbing the wall at times. It felt like he was getting his sea legs back in descending a few floors.

He stepped out into late afternoon on a drowned world, a cosmopolitan city of canals crossed by foot-bridges, muggy air capped with solid cloud cover.[113] Three ring canals: Agracht and Bogracht divided the social classes; Cogracht surrounded the city with docks on the city side and shantytowns on the other side.[114] William walked along the Bogracht, crossed the Bridge of Flies, and turned a corner onto the Xochimlico,[115] where he entered the Glory Hole, a barroom frequented by expatri-ates.[116]

The place inside offered dingy daylit gloom without any of the glamour afforded by night's veil. Peopled by heavy drinkers and shady characters, able bodies being destroyed through idle sloth.

Thoris[117] looked up from his station behind the bar.

---

113. By early September, 1951, Mexico City had been swamped by the aftermath of Hurricane Dog.

114. The city's circular canal plan evokes a design given for fabled Atlantis, while the main canal names sound like utilitarian Esperanto.

115. Xochimlico: A canal area of Mexico City.

116. Glory Hole: Named after a mining term and based on the Bounty bar.

117. Thoris: A Swedish surname. On the ERB fiction side, an allusion to Dejah Thoris, the princess of Mars; on the WSB biography side, his role seems that of John Healy, co-owner of the Bounty bar.

"Howdy, Bill. Rather early. Vhat Ay can get for you?"[118]

"I am looking to sell my gun."

"Not the Lemon Squeezer?"[119]

"That is the one."

"She is a beaut," said the Swede.

"Yep. But I need the cash. We are looking to pull up stakes, head back to the States."

"Oh, is that it? You bane good to me, and Ay vill be sorry to see you go. Ay tank Ay know a fellow who might be interested in your gun. You able to meet him tonight?"

"That would be wonderful."

"All right, then. Bring the vife to the little party, and maybe hay vill tak the pistol."

"Your place, at seven."

"No, over at the old pagan temple in the A-ring — you savvy?"

"Sure. Say, this is some kind of soiree you are planning."

"You bat. Hired to set up for an artsy event over there."

•

William, loath to return to the lair of the hag, had time to kill. He wandered the canals, wondering through a miscellany. Along the Giudecca[120] he thought of getting

---

118. Swedish form of spoken English drawn from the sailor Anderssen found in *The Beasts of Tarzan* (serialized 1914).

119. Lemon Squeezer: A common nickname for the Smith & Wesson Safety Hammerless, on account of how the break-open exposes the entire five-chambered cylinder in a way that visually resembles a kitchen tool for juicing citrus fruits.

120. Giudecca: A canal of Venice, Italy.

food for dinner, and pondered the mysterious lack of fresh fish in a water town. He imagined fishwives touting trays of silvery fish with heads like roses. Even octopus would be preferable to the black centipedes, but there was no choice in the matter.

As he shuffled alongside the Moyka[121] he struggled to recall the name of his almost-conquest. Not Joanne; that was his daughter, of the same age.[122] He mused that he never learned the Gibson Girl's name, but there were moments in her presence when he felt as though he were floating, and she seemed to have a similar joy, too.

He stopped at a meat stall on Altair.[123] No sign of beef, chicken, or mutton. Not even any iguana. He bought a couple segments of raw centipede. And gin for the hag, always the gin.

With heavy feet he mounted the stairs. In the room he woke the hag and set her to making dinner. She complained about the meat, but he claimed it was just like lobster tail. In retaliation she contrived to panfry them in such a way that they were burnt on the outside and nearly raw at the center.

When he told her about the soiree, she raised a fuss, swearing she would never walk all the way there. She demanded a gondola or a sedan chair. He stomped out to find one.

---

121. Moyka: A canal of St. Petersburg, Russia.

122. Joanne: ERB's daughter Joan (pronounced "Jo-ann") was the same age as his second wife, Florence. In fact, the two women had been friends; they never spoke after the wedding.

123. Altair: A canal of Venice, California, extant circa 1905–29.

5 ALONG THE MAZY CANALS

Back outside he found afternoon giving way to evening with still no glimpse of sky. To the left about twenty yards away, a short jetty poked out into the canal. Next to the jetty stood a hiring stand. Across the wide sidewalk from the booth towered a building whose ground floor shop showed a sign emblazoned with a sedan chair. Although William and his wife had been staying in the city for months, he had no idea how much these taxi services might cost. He adjusted his batwing tie, straightened his white linen coat, and strolled over to the gondola stand.

The attendant there gave him a warm smile.

"Would the foreign dignitary be inclined to take passage by gondola?"

"Perhaps," said William. "How much would it cost to get a ride for two to the old temple at A-ring? One way."

"Such a fare would be one hundred."

William gave an involuntary jerk. The absurdity of his situation became clear: he was trying to sell his pistol, with the hope of raising five hundred, and yet this one frivolous canoe-ride would take a large portion of that.

"Perhaps not this evening," said the attendant with mild sympathy.

"No, thank you," said William. He turned on his heel and strolled stiffly down the block toward the sedan chair station. The counterman there saw him coming, then returned to reading his newspaper.

William arrived at the counter.

Moments passed.

"Hello," said William.

The counterman nodded without looking up.

"I would like to hire a chair."

"I doubt it," said the other, turning a page.

"What is the fare, from here to the old temple at A-ring?"

"'A-ring'?"

"Agracht."

"A chair for you?"

"For my wife."

"And you will walk?"

"That is right."

"Fifty. In advance."

"Thank you," said William through gritted teeth. "I will consider."

"I doubt it."

William left the shop. The next door down was a tavern called The Canal Man. In the waterway across the pavement from this establishment a young pole man stood guard in a modest gondola. His body language suggested he was dejected and bored.

William walked over and said, "Hello there. Why so sad?"

"Good evening, sir. I need money for my girl, and I am set out here to watch the boat while the others are inside."

"Ah, poor and lonely. How many are there?"

"Three."

"So many! And you must share the money with them."

"That is so."

"Tell me, would they notice if you were to take a quick ride to Agracht?"

The youth considered, and then said, "Maybe not. Where on Agracht?"

"The old temple."

The youth smiled. "Yes, that might work."

"And you would keep all the money."

"How much?"

"Twenty."

"Make it thirty-five."

"But you will get it all."

"At the beginning I will."

"Here is twenty-five. Take it."

The young man shook his head impishly.

"All right. Thirty."

The pole man took the money.

"I will meet you at the hotel up there."

"Why not get in right now? We must hurry."

"I have to get my wife."

"What, another? You tricked me!"

"Now, now, it will be fine. Watch for me."

•

The fetching of the hag proved challenging for William. First she would not believe he had hired a gondola; then she wasted valuable time on attempts to make herself more presentable; finally he pulled her out of the room and down the stairs.

When she saw the craft she expressed her displeasure through a sharp jab into her husband's side.

William silently acknowledged her point. The gondola was off, somehow. It only had one chair, and this facing a long raised bench on the centerline. William offered her the seat, and placed himself on the bench facing her. It was awkwardly close and their knees bumped together.

The gondola shot ahead.

William felt eyes upon him. Glancing around he found their sources, citizens expressing consternation, bemusement, and distaste. He wondered aloud if it was their seating arrangement. The hag told him to turn around on the bench and sit cross-legged, to form a lap for her head. He did so as she moved to lie down upon the bench.

"Already they stare upon us," she said, "and that chair is too hard and straight."

The gondola flitted suddenly around a corner into a back alley type of canal. A place of silence, mildew, stagnant waters, and cloying weeds.

"If only we could see the Moon," said the hag. "Have we ever seen the Moon here?"

They emerged onto the canal Agracht and slowed to a somber speed. William heard a piano playing off in the distance, what sounded like a church song. Voices sang, a violin joined, and then came a banjo. It gained speed into a Sousa march with minstrel flourishes, and he recognized "A Hot Time in the Old Town Tonight."

"Why the sigh, Half-Moon Face?"

"That song," he said.

"What about it? I like it."

"They probably think it is the American anthem."[124]

"Almost there, mister. Get ready."

"Come on, Joan. Sit up."

"Not until we dock."

The moment the boat touched the sidewalk the hag sat bolt upright. A scream and a curse burst from the strollers. William helped the hag up out of the gondola and the pole man rushed away as if propelled by the muttering of the crowd. Suddenly Thoris was there, a puzzled smile on his Swedish face.

---

124. anthem: During the Spanish-American War (1898), "A Hot Time in the Old Town Tonight" was used as a theme by Teddy Roosevelt's Rough Riders to such effect that the Spaniards in Cuba thought it was the U.S. national anthem (C.A. Browne, *The Story of Our National Ballads,* p. 208).

"A hearse you tak? Such a queer cutup. Follow me now, let us go in."

6 AT THE OLD TEMPLE

Thoris led them past the cyclopean columns, then along the side of the dark Pelasgian temple to an entrance near the rear. Entering the threshold, they followed him down a dark hallway lit at infrequent intervals by lanterns.

"Up ahead is the gallery," said Thoris. "We yust go through an' upstairs."

"Is the buyer here yet?"

"You bat."

After a turn to the right they came into a large room with paintings leaning on the walls prior to hanging. The art showed a variety of styles and subjects, yet shared an unsettling power. In one a Primitivist Prometheus offered his own steaming heart to light the sun. Another depicted a kitchen where a beaming woman put a baby's arm into the bubbling kettle. A third showed a group of cephaloid surgeons performing a vivisection upon a talking white man.

At the other side of the room they went up some wooden stairs that doubled back to a floor above the gallery, but this place was surprisingly like a rundown room in a flea-bitten hotel. William was flummoxed, as if this whole evening journey had been in a circle.

There was a couch with two men, a coffee table cluttered with empty booze bottles, and a couple of chairs. When the men looked back over their shoulders to see the newcomers, William recognized Kamurder on the left.

William strode to the coffee table, took out his pistol, and set it down among the dead soldiers.

"There he is. A good gun that got me out of a couple of tight spots."

"You know guns well, Mr. Lee?"

"Sure. They're tools. You know, I would like to move to South America with the wife and kids, get a homestead where we could live off the land. Killing and eating the wild boars that are everywhere down there."

The hag cackled and said, "With Bill as our hunter, we would starve to death."

William felt eyes upon him, the eyes of a vast crowd far larger than the four others in the room. He took up the pistol.

"Show the boys what kind of a shot old Bill is," he said. "Finish your gin and put the glass on your head. I will snap it off from across the room."

She put the glass on her head. She turned away with a giggle, saying, "I cannot look — you know I cannot stand the sight of blood . . ."[125]

William took a few paces away from her, turned, and raised the pistol. He thought, *I will shoot that glass and prove myself.* But then he thought, *I will shoot you, teach you a lesson, and free myself to escape with Florence*[126] — *we will fly the night sky*

---

125. This version of events follows the scenario depicted in James Grauerholz and Ira Silverberg (editors), *Word Virus: The William S. Burroughs Reader*, p. 41–42.

126. Florence: ERB's second wife, Florence Gilbert, a silent film star who came with two children from her previous marriage. Her marriage to ERB lasted six years. It seems likely that ERB had first admired her in films. She was in dozens of features and

to Hawaii on an airboat.[127] As his finger began to tighten, he thought, *No, my darling, one for you and one for me, then we will awaken on Earth together.*

The hammer fell with a click.

William found he could not move. His arm was frozen. He was a living statue.

"You see," said Kamurder in a loud lecture hall voice, "the subject had a belief that if he executed his spouse and killed himself he would return to his plane of origin, his 'home world.' This might be true on the surface of Jizma, but it is certainly false in the Intersphere."

A tittering twittering round of applause came from beyond the walls.

"Now that the subject has been disabused of his hope, now that he comprehends it as a horror to be avoided, we will go again and make him follow through with it. This time the gun will be loaded, and this time he will shoot her dead.

"Hark, I hear the Haunted Pipes of Lem . . ."

There was a sound like panpipes that rose in volume until there was nothing else in the universe.

When you hear that the preaching ridge of Dreams where they joined the bend down low for to drive away screams came from behind them. Lee and when you gets religion, you want directly overhead, now raining down. There'll be a hot time in the old town tonight, my baby[128]

---

shorts from 1920 to 1927, but "Hello from Heaven" is not listed as one of them.

127. to Hawaii on an airboat: While in 1935 the newlyweds took a cruise ship from Los Angeles to Hawaii (Porges, p. 572), it was in 1937 that they flew by airboat from Los Angeles to Hawaii on their way to China (Danton Burroughs, *ERBzine* 0890).

128. An example of the cutup technique, this time folding in lyrics from the song "A Hot Time in the Old Town" (1896).

7 ALONG THE CANAL MAZE

Back outside he found afternoon crawling along. He glanced to the left, where a short jetty marked the place to hire gondolas and sedan chairs.

"Forget it," he muttered. "Save the money."

He loosened his batwing tie and started his hike.

William strolled along the Bogracht with a new sense of relief that he would be leaving soon. As he crossed the Bridge of Flies he felt a weird sense of future nostalgia. He asked himself what would come next, what would he do back in the United States, and he admitted he did not know: it was joy enough to imagine simply not being anymore in the wretched lagoon.

He walked through the business area of the city, passing a butcher shop (having black meat[129] only, alas), a bakery, a bodega,[130] a bill collection agency, a barber shop, a

---

129. black meat: Reference to *Naked Lunch* (Ch. 6) section "black meat."

130. bodega: (Spanish) A small grocery store in a city; a wineshop, wine cellar, or barroom.

boteco,[131] a boutique, a beauty parlor, and a bank. He crossed the Agracht on the crumbling Bridge of Dreams, and joined the parade of strollers making their daily promenade around the city's finest.

Approaching the old temple, he saw Thoris sitting against one of the cyclopean columns. The Swede stood and walked over to meet him.

"Vhat, no vife?"

"She could not make it."

"Too bad. Follow me."

William followed Thoris past the columns, then along the side of the dark Pelasgian temple to a side entrance near the rear. Once through the threshold, they went down a dark hallway lit at infrequent intervals by lanterns.

"Up ahead is the gallery," said Thoris. "We yust go through an' upstairs."

"Is the buyer here yet?"

"You bat."

"I hope to get five hundred."

"That much?"

"Help me out and I will give you a commission."

Thoris grunted at that.

After a turn to the right they came into a large room with paintings leaning on the walls prior to hanging. The art seemed uncanny. At the other side of the room they went up some wooden stairs that doubled back to a floor above the gallery, but this place was surprisingly like a rundown room of a flea-bitten hotel. William was flummoxed, as if he had unwittingly traveled in a circle.

There was a couch with two men, a coffee table cluttered with empty booze bottles, and a couple of chairs. When the men looked back over their shoulders to see the newcomers, William recognized Kamurder on the left.

William strode to the coffee table and said, "Hello, I

---

131. boteco: (Brazilian Portuguese) A pub or barroom.

am William."

"Bill," said Kamurder, "this is Marc. Old college friend."

William took out his pistol, and set it down among the dead soldiers.

"And this is Lemon Squeezer. A good gun that got me out of a couple of tight spots."

"You know guns well, Mr. Lee?"

"Sure. They're tools. You know, I would like to move to South America with the wife and kids, get a homestead where we could live off the land. Killing and eating the wild boars that are everywhere down there."

"You have children, Mr. Lee?"

"Yes, three. A girl and two boys."

"You would not hunt boar with the Squeezer."

"No, no. Get a Winchester for that."

"That is a lot of boar — three meals a day."

"A regular lord of the forest!"[132]

A piping flute sound came from outside.

"What is that?" asked Marc, looking around.

"Knife sharpener," said William. He took up his pistol, placed it in his pocket. "Excuse me a few minutes." He went out the door, started down the stairs.

"Vait," called Thoris, trying to catch up. "Vair you are going?"

William stopped in the gallery when Thoris was close and said, "I will get my knife sharpened. Talk up the price for me. Earn a commission."

Heading toward the side entrance, William wondered how they had heard the pipes from within a stone edifice. The tune had sounded as clear as it did through the flimsy walls of his hotel.

When he stepped outside he heard the sound again. There was something archaic in the music, something

---

132. lord of the forest: A reference to Tarzan.

strangely familiar, very old and very sad. Shepherd music played on a bamboo flute like a panpipe; pre-classical, Pelasgian perhaps.[133]

William followed the music to the alley behind the temple. He found a line of people waiting, cooks and scullery maids. William waited in line. The women mentioned that in ancient times the temple was always in need of knife sharpening. He admitted he had only the one pocketknife, but nobody offered him cuts in the line. The women went back to their gossip. After another ten minutes, William left the knife with the sharpener and promised to be back later.[134]

Upon returning to the side entrance, William heard a hubbub out at the front, a few screams and some yelling. So he went to reconnoiter, but found nothing to see when he got there. He tried asking a few people and one man told him a prank had been committed.

William checked his pocket watch, learning it was one thirty.[135]

A lot of people were going into the temple's front entrance, and William went along with the flow. Past the cyclopean columns he entered the vast cavernous room lit by radium bulbs. The ceiling was high, ornate with designs,

---

133. Close to a passage by WSB in *The Yage Letters Redux:* "There is something archaic in this music strangely familiar, very old and very sad. . . . Shepherd music played on a bamboo instrument like a panpipe, pre-classic, Etruscan perhaps. . . . Atlantean?" (p. 14). Such a haunting sound appears repeatedly in *The Ticket That Exploded* (i.e, Ch. 2, 8, 14, 15, 16, and 20).

134. On the day in question, WSB heard the piping of the knife sharpener out on the street at around 3 PM and left a knife to be sharpened (Miles, p. 206).

135. 1:30 PM: Joan arrived at the party at 1 PM or at 3 PM. (Ibid).

but there were no windows at all.

There was a stage, where a dramatic play was already in progress. A man sat in a chair across from a couch bearing the most beautiful woman in the world.

"You have children, madam?"

"Yes, four. Three boys and a girl."

"That is curious. Your husband said you had three."

"Maybe he is not counting the one I had before I met him."

"Ah, so you had three with your second husband?"

"That is right. Alex, Cleo-Sel, and Ptolemy-Phil."[136]

"He said your three children were Joanne, Herbert, and John."[137]

"That is absurd. He must have been joking."

"He calls you Emma,[138] or Joan,[139] but I call you by your true name, Cleopatra, because I am Marc Antony."

"No, you could not be . . . ?"

"Remember, Cleo. We had our pact. I woke up here. And now I have found you again."

"No, my husband will come soon!"

"My friend is guarding the door."

"Wait, wait! Tell me more."

"We are here. We have bodies. There is food. There are pleasures. This is not Hades."

"No, it is not."

"I believe we were deified by our peoples, and this is the Elysian Fields or the Blessed Isles."

---

136. These are Cleopatra's children.

137. These are ERB's children by Emma. The daughter's name was spelled "Joan" but pronounced "Jo-ann."

138. Emma: Wife of ERB.

139. Joan: Wife of WSB; the written name of ERB's daughter.

8 THE CLIMAX BATTLE

Ahead William saw a half-lit chamber. It appeared to be an unfinished storage room with a simple wooden pillar at the center. He entered slowly, leading with his pistol.

There was a whoosh from the left and something metal struck the pistol from his hand. He sidled to the right and the machete came at him again, missing this time. With surprise William Lee recognized the assailant as his old enemy Koyotel, in the flesh instead of working through a ridden zombie.

Lee suddenly realized he was not on Earth, and with that shock came memories of the Intersphere.

Koyotel swung a chest-cleaving blow but he dodged it by a hair. He moved toward the pistol on the floor and dodged again, taking a burning cut on the cheek.

Lee snatched up the revolver and now Koyotel used a blocking strike to halt the rising barrel from pointing at her. Lee fired but the shot missed.

Koyotel swung at his head and he parried with the pistol. With the blade and gun locked together, Lee tried to force the machete down. He fired but missed. Fired again to a click.

Koyotel, triumphant at this turn, suddenly surged with

bestial fury. She drew the blade back and with a scream brought down a lethal strike. When Lee dodged it, the machete sank deep into the wooden pillar.

As she tried to pull the machete free, Lee whipped the pistol across her face with a devastating blow. Staggering back, she drew a stiletto. Another pistol-whip caused her eye to swell up.

She stabbed at him but missed. He hammered at her head, then took her knife and slit her throat, ending it.

Panting, Lee found his recollection of the Intersphere had a big gap in the transition from his airborne ride to his residence in the city of Gnydon. He pushed these puzzles aside before crossing the room and going up the stairs.

"Hark," said a voice, "what is this? The beleaguered cuckold enters, already redolent with the pungent aroma of cordite. He has prematurely shot his load. That is no way to enter the defiled bridal chamber . . ."

Lee felt invisible hands place something heavy in his jacket pocket. He reached in and drew out a box of bullets.

"Time to reload."

Lee started to put the box back but then his body moved on its own: sitting down, it unloaded the spent brass from the revolver, and then inserted fresh bullets from the box.

•

The seedy room was crowded with eager watchers. There were insect people, vampires, dwarfs,[140] a few blue urbans and several yellow nomads. Kamurder was there next to a giant coiled eel monster dotted with eyes. The crowd parted before Lee, creating a straight way to the

---

140. insect people, vampires, dwarfs: WSB denizens of the Interzone. More completely, "Insect People of Minraud," vampires, and "Death Dwarfs."

couch where Marc was on top of a woman.[141]

Lee felt rage. He raised the pistol to aim. But then he resisted. He felt his arm lock in place. He strained, moisture running down his face, but he could not move his arm. His finger began tightening on the trigger. His body broke into a sweat as he threw his entire energy into resisting. His finger continued to squeeze.[142]

Just as the pistol fired, a man leapt forward from the right. He looked a lot like Lee, and the bullet caught him straight in the chest.

Suddenly the spell broke: Lee could move. The room erupted in gunfire all around as the yellow men began killing the watchers. Lee moved to shield a crouching Ayssa against threats. Marc was already down. Lee shot the eel four times, kicked a dwarf, and pistol-whipped an insect man.

As he fled with Ayssa through the temple, Lee felt more memories unlock, revealing the amphibians who had

---

141. Caught in the act: The first reports from Mexico City newspapers suggested that WSB shot his wife Joan in jealousy. In an academic paper decades later, James W. Grauerholz writes "One uncorroborated source (Graham Seidman. . . .) even suggests . . . that perhaps Burroughs had surprised [Joan and her lover] *in flagrante*" ("The Death of Joan Vollmer Burroughs: What Really Happened?" p. 62). Candidates for Joan's lover include John Healy, co-owner of the Bounty bar, and Lucien Carr, an American friend who had visited Joan while WSB was away hunting yage (Miles, p. 203). Note that Carr had served time for manslaughter committed in 1944.

142. Controlled by another: WSB said in a 1980 interview, "You see, I've always felt myself to be controlled at some times by this completely malevolent force . . . the Ugly Spirit . . . [that fateful day] I knew that the Ugly Spirit . . . would take over, and that something awful would happen" (Miles, p. 207).

found him in the swamp.[143] Yes, they had shot down his gasbag, expecting to find the sage Kamurder. The amphibians were Sacrilegious, waging their war against the gods. Gnydon city had formerly been theirs.

Outside the temple, the cloud cover was gone, exposing the leprous sun of the Intersphere. Humanoid screams spread panic as invading tower machines strode in from the C-ring.

Holding hands, Lee and Ayssa ran to the Bridge of Dreams where they joined the stampeding mass trying to cross. A new wave of screams came from behind them. Lee looked back to see that a burning cloud had formed overhead, and it was raining down drops of fire. This curtain of flame was fast approaching. Lee knew they could not outrun it.

The crowd's jostling pushed humanoids off the edges to fall into the canal. Lee saw a mad hope there and dragged Ayssa over toward the side. She screamed and resisted. The flamedrops began burning people at the foot of the bridge. Lee jerked Ayssa into his arms and launched himself over the side.

They splashed into the filthy water and he pulled her along under the bridge. Here they were safe from the raining fire.

"The machines — up there," gasped Lee. "Our friends — amphibians."

"Danger — in between — the twain," said she.

The pounding of the ground continued, the footsteps of the approaching tower machines. From the bridge

---

143. memories unlock: In ERB's *Tarzan and the Jewels of Opar* (serialized 1916), for most of the novel the mighty ape-man wanders in an amnesic idyll, returned to his pre-married state, while Jane is kidnapped, threatened, and fought over. Aside from hinting at marital discord within ERB's life, this plot shows a daring psychological experimentation.

above, the screams gave way to moaning.

The rain stopped and the shadow of the cloud retreated. Lee and Ayssa scrambled up the far side of the canal. Turning away from the dead and dying, the couple hurried to follow the living. Lee glanced back to see the cloud narrowed and stretched down to touch the ground, forming a giant column of vapor.

In the other direction four fighting machines were coming on at a jog. Each had two legs and a long tail.[144] Lee and Ayssa ran toward them. Looking over his shoulder Lee saw the vapor column had solidified into a giant humanoid one hundred and fifty feet tall, with the crowned head of a vulture, wings instead of arms, and the bent legs of a gorilla. It was eating the wounded and growing stronger with each bone-breaking bite.

---

144. two legs and a long tail: An allusion to the Martian tripods of H.G. Wells's *The War of the Worlds* (1898).

EPILOGUE

"What happened next?!" I cried when their telling halted.

"We do not know," said the flickerman known as K-9.[145]

"This be the reason for our visit," said the bluebeard. "We hope ye can tell us."

"What? How could I tell you?"

"Perhaps you have seen a pattern in all we have said," said K-9, "and could guess where he would go next."

"Tell us," said the quiet old red man. "Have you seen William Lee?"

"No! Has he returned to Earth?"

"We do not know."

"Wait," I said. "How are you here?"

"We cannot explain it."

"Have you visited Alexandria?"

"Yes."

---

145. K-9: Character K9 is an agent in the Nova Trilogy. It is not clear which side he is on. On the ERB side, number-names are used for the synthetic men of Mars, e.g., "Tor-dur-bar," which means "four million and eight."

"Then you found the tomb?"

"Yes. We arrived there. The bodies are absent."

"So that means they must have returned to Earth."

"Not necessarily. The bodies could have been stolen by treasure hunters."

"Norman, have you seen William Lee?"

"No, I have not."

"Our search continues then, in this world and others."

The flickerman gave me a salute and then disappeared before my eyes.

The sage smiled ruefully, scratched his bluebeard, and vanished.

The last visitor said, "Keep this as a memento of our visit."

He gave me an uncanny thing, then vanished like the others.

And so I found myself alone in my living room, holding the artifact, as dawn's early light touched the windowpanes.

APPENDIX

UNDER THE MOONS OF JIZMA

Ch.	ERB	WSB	Other
For.	PM for.		
Pref.	PM 1		The Raven
1	PM 1	NL app.	The Waste Land
2	PM 1, 2		Heart of Darkness
3	MM 1	NL 4	
4	MM 2		The Golden Ass
5	PM	NL 16	Heart of Darkness
6	PM	NL 9	
7	LG		She
8			
9	PM 27		Midsummer Night's
10	PM 27		
11	PM 28		

LG = Llana of Gathol (Mars #10)
MM = Master Mind of Mars (Mars #6)
NL = Naked Lunch
PM = A Princess of Mars (Mars #1)

THE GODS OF JIZMA

Ch.	ERB	WSB	Other
Intro.	FM for.		
1		SM 2	Innocents Abroad
2	GM 18	TTE 3, 8	The Waste Land
3		TTE 12, 15, 1	Hamlet
4	GM 4, 5	NL app.	lotus eaters
5	GM 22	TTE 11	Georgic IV
Epilog	GM 23	SM 7	

FM = Fighting Man of Mars (Mars #7)

126

GM = The Gods of Mars (Mars #2)
NL = Naked Lunch
SM = Soft Machine (Nova #1)
TTE = The Ticket That Exploded (Nova #2)

SECRET MASTER OF JIZMA

Ch.	ERB	WSB	Other
Intro.	GM fore.		The Raven, Roosevelt
1	GM 23, AEC 1		
2	AEC 2	NL Interzone	Bluebeard
3		biography 1944	Snow White
4	biography 1934	biography 1951	Atlantis
5			Hot Time
6	biography 1934	biography 1951	
7			Panpipes
8	TJO 22		War of the Worlds
Epilog			

AEC = At the Earth's Core
GM = The Gods of Mars
TJO = Tarzan and the Jewels of Opar

BIBLIOGRAPHY

Primary

Burroughs, Edgar Rice. *A Princess of Mars* (serialized 1912).
———. *The Gods of Mars* (serialized 1913).
———. *At the Earth's Core* (serialized 1914).
———. *The Master Mind of Mars* (1928).

Burroughs, William S. *Naked Lunch* (1959).
———. *The Soft Machine* (1961).
———. *The Ticket That Exploded* (1962).
———. *The Nova Express* (1964).

Secondary

Burroughs, Edgar Rice. *The Beasts of Tarzan* (serialized 1914).
———. *Tarzan and the Jewels of Opar* (serialized 1916).
———. *Thuvia, Maid of Mars* (serialized 1916).
———. *The Girl from Hollywood* (1923).
———. *The Master Mind of Mars* (1928).
———. *Synthetic Men of Mars* (1940).
———. *Llana of Gathol* (serialized 1941).
———. *John Carter of Mars* (1964).
Burroughs, William S. *Exterminator!* (1966).
Coleridge, Samuel Taylor. "Kubla Khan" (1816).
Conrad, Joseph. *Heart of Darkness* (1899).
———. *Nostromo* (1904).
Eliot, T.S. "The Waste Land" (1922).
Fowles, John. *The Magus* (1965).
Haggard, H. Rider. *She* (1887).
Homer. *The Odyssey*.
Poe, Edgar Allan. "Ligeia" (1838).
———. "The Raven" (1845).
———. "Annabel Lee" (1849).

Shakespeare, William. *A Midsummer Night's Dream* (c1595).
————. *The Tragedy of Hamlet, Prince of Denmark* (c1600).
————. *Antony and Cleopatra* (c1607).
Twain, Mark. *The Innocents Abroad* (1869).
Vergil. *Georgics* (29 B.C.). Translation by Greenough, from his *Bucolics, Aeneid, and Georgics of Vergil* (1900).
Wells, H. G. *The War of the Worlds* (1898).

Non-fiction

Browne, C.A. *The Story of Our National Ballads.* Thomas Y. Crowell Co.: New York, 1919.
Burroughs, Danton. "Florence Gilbert Burroughs" (Part I). *Bill & Sue-On Hillman's ERBzine* Issue 0890. <http://www.erbzine.com/mag8/0890.html>. Accessed 15 September 2017.
Burroughs, William and Allen Ginsberg. *The Yage Letters Redux.* City Lights Books: San Francisco, 2006.
Grauerholz, James W. "The Death of Joan Vollmer Burroughs: What Really Happened?" American Studies: University of Kansas, 2002.
Lupoff, Richard A. *Master of Adventure: The Worlds of Edgar Rice Burroughs.* University of Nebraska Press: Lincoln, Nebraska, 2005.
Miles, Barry. *Call Me Burroughs: A Life.* Hachette Book Group: New York, 2014.
Porges, Irwin. *Edgar Rice Burroughs: The Man Who Created Tarzan.* Brigham Young University Press: Provo, Utah, 1975.
Roy, John Flint. *A Guide to Barsoom.* Ballantine Books: New York, 1976.
Skerl, Jennie. *William S. Burroughs.* Twayne's United States authors series; TUSAS 438. Twayne Publishers: Boston, c1985.

ABOUT THE AUTHOR

Michael Andre-Driussi has seen a few dozen of his stories published in such places as *Perihelion SF, M-Brane SF,* and *Stupefying Stories Showcase.* Many of these fictions have been collected in *Fallout Stories* (2016), *Doomsday and Other Tours* (2016), and *Old Flames Burn Manvi* (2017).